PENGUIN BOOKS

THE TASTE OF A MAN

Slavenka Drakulić was born in Croatia in 1949. She is the author of several books of non-fiction, including *Deadly Sins of Feminism*; *How We Survived Communism and Even Laughed*; *Balkan Express: Fragments from the Other Side of War*; and, most recently, *Café Europa: Life After Communism*. She is also the author of two previous novels: *Holograms of Fear*, which was a bestseller in Yugoslavia and was shortlisted for the Best Foreign Book Award by *The Independent* (UK), and *Marble Skin*. Drakulić's prose has been compared to that of Marguerite Duras, Samuel Beckett, and Albert Camus. Her books have been published in thirteen countries and translated into twelve languages.

Drakulić is a freelance journalist and novelist who contributes regularly to *The Nation*, *The New Republic*, *La Stampa* (Italy), *Dagens Nyheter* (Sweden), and *Frankfurter Rundschau* (Germany), among other international newspapers and magazines. She divides her time between Sweden, Austria, and Croatia.

The Taste
of a Man

SLAVENKA DRAKULIĆ

Translated by
CHRISTINA PRIBICHEVICH ZORIC

PENGUIN BOOKS

PENGUIN BOOKS

Published by the Penguin Group

Penguin Books USA Inc., 375 Hudson Street,
New York, New York 10014, U.S.A.

Penguin Books Ltd, 27 Wrights Lane, London W8 5TZ, England
Penguin Books Australia Ltd, Ringwood, Victoria, Australia
Penguin Books Canada Ltd, 10 Alcorn Avenue,
Toronto, Ontario, Canada M4V 3B2
Penguin Books (N.Z.) Ltd, 182–190 Wairau Road,
Auckland 10, New Zealand

Penguin Books Ltd, Registered Offices:
Harmondsworth, Middlesex, England

First published in Great Britain by Abacus,
a division of Little, Brown and Company (UK) 1997
Published in Penguin Books 1997

1   3   5   7   9   10   8   6   4   2

PUBLISHER'S NOTE
This is a work of fiction. Names, characters, places, and incidents
either are the product of the author's imagination or are used
fictitiously, and any resemblance to actual persons, living or dead,
events, or locales is entirely coincidental.

ISBN 0 14 02.6622 4
CIP data available

Printed in the United States of America
Set in Baskerville

'You must sit down,' says Love, 'and taste my meat.'
  So I did sit and eat.

George Herbert, *Love* (III)

I

There is nothing I hate more than house-cleaning, but these past three days before Christmas I have hardly done anything else. I spent almost twenty dollars on various kinds of liquids and powders to clean the floors in the kitchen, hall, bedroom and living room, the bathroom tiles, bathtub, toilet and sink. I bought a spray to wash the windows and a paste to clean the brass doorknobs. My diligence was such that I even dipped a damp cloth in Ajax and wiped down the plastic-coated wallpaper in the bedroom. The apartment smells like a hospital. The unpleasant odour of chlorine and ammonia will linger in the corners for days after I am gone. I am sure it has killed off all the cockroaches. I could hardly sleep myself last night, even though, in defiance of the cold, I had left the front window wide open.

The smell reminds me of our apartment in Warsaw the first day or two after Jadwiga had finished with it. Of course, she used to say that you start cleaning an apartment from the table down, not from the floor up. That is probably why she washed the dishes first, which, I must admit, this time I did not do. Once a week she would come all the way from Pawlowice to clean our apartment in Czarnlecklego Street

1

and all day long I would listen to the roll of her heavy peasant body around the apartment, leaving the sour smell of sweat in its wake.

I am afraid neither Jadwiga nor my mother would understand that this time the floors had to be done first. I had to start with the pinewood floorboards in the bedroom which someone long ago had painted a dark brown. Only then came the living room, and after that the hall, the bathroom and finally the kitchen and the table.

The most important thing, I felt, was to decide the order in which to clean the apartment so that I could plan how much time I would need. And since this was going to be a major operation, it could not all be done in one day. I figured that if I organized myself properly, four days should be enough.

Ever since I had started living on my own in the apartment of my late Aunt Ana, my father's sister, because, as a research assistant at Warsaw University's Institute for Literature, I could not afford to rent, I had cleaned the place twice a month and tried to be systematic about it. When I cleaned, the same picture often flashed through my mind: at the day's end, when Jadwiga had already changed back into her street clothes, my mother would walk over to the painting hanging above the piano, run her finger along the frame, look at her finger and then at Jadwiga. Jadwiga would quietly watch the ritual. She knew it by heart. She knew that it would be followed by a displeased frown on that fine face with its frame of blonde hair, but that my mother would then shrug her shoulders, like a child suddenly bored with its game. Jadwiga, however, continued to do things her own way. My mother set great store by cleanliness, discipline, order and control. Sometimes I think I inherited some of that from her.

When my mother died of breast cancer, Jadwiga wept for her like a daughter. The disease must have dragged on for more than the three years we knew about it, but in the end she still went suddenly somehow, in a matter of weeks. Long afterwards the apartment still carried a trace of the perfume my father used to bring her from his trips abroad. He was hardly ever at home – he was a pianist. I say 'was' because after my mother's death he stopped giving concerts. He gives only lessons now, and even those grudgingly, just so as not to be alone. My mother played the cello in her youth. She was talented, their friends say, but when I came along she took a job in a school and that was the end of her musical career. It is hard for me to judge whether she was content with her life; I do not think it was a question she ever asked herself. She was very reserved and did not like to talk about herself. As a child I played the piano, too, of course, and every time my father returned from a long trip I would have to show him the progress I had made. But since he was never particularly enthusiastic about it, I soon realized that I was playing the piano largely to please him, not because my future lay in that direction.

I had two responsibilities as a child: to play the piano and to pray. My mother did not ask me to go to church every day as she did, just on Sundays like my father. I remember when I was very little my father said that there was no point in making me go, that I could decide for myself once I grew up. So I was surprised to learn two years ago that my father had gone back to daily prayer. But when I was a child I knelt down by my bed every evening, shivering – our apartment was never warm enough. And as I prayed, the hardness of the floor would press against my knees and the parquet joinings dug into my flesh. There was no rug on that spot. My mother would not let me pull one over to the bed: she said surely I could stand the floor for a few moments. And I did not find it difficult, because I was not alone when I prayed. She would kneel down beside me and pray for me. That was the only moment in the entire day when we were together, completely alone, just the two of us. Then, and only then, I felt protected, because of the warm nearness of her body, because of the fervour with which she prayed, omitting from the prayer herself, my father, the whole world, everybody except me.

So I drew up a schedule for cleaning the rooms in this New York apartment, only slightly bigger than my place in Warsaw, and tried not to forget such seemingly unimportant details as the knobs and the doors, because you can tell from the doors what condition the house may be in. All the furniture in all the rooms had to be cleaned, the kitchen cupboards washed inside and out, the refrigerator defrosted and the old gas stove restored to some kind of order. Ajax liquid, spray and powder seemed to be the best tools for the job. I also placed my trust in plain vinegar and diluted chlorine. This time I was absolutely positive I could not over-clean. I even took two bedroom rugs to the dry cleaner's, completely unnecessarily. When I first moved into the apartment I found them rolled up in a corner and decided not to bother with them for my one semester in New York. But there were a few dark brown bloodstains on the floor near the rugs and I could not be sure that there were not any on the rugs themselves. I wanted to eliminate any possibility of doubt. First I washed the stains on the floor, soaking them with plain cold water, and then I scrubbed them out with diluted ammonia, which immediately alleviated the sweetish stench of blood coming from the bathroom, a smell I have had to live with these last four days in New York.

This was not my first encounter with the smell of death.

The three of us were in New York five years ago, when my mother had been admitted to Sloan-Kettering. I remember that my father and I got off two subway stations too soon and had to walk some distance to the hospital. It was summer, the asphalt stuck to our shoes and the entire city smelled of rot and decay. I had been feeling nauseous for days. I refused to leave the air-conditioned apartment until I accepted the fact that this was the smell of the city, the smell of New York in summer. I think that of all New York, the only thing I remembered about that visit was its smell.

Two years later, just a few days before the end, when she was lying in hospital in Warsaw, only occasionally conscious, I think Mama sensed that smell and that it bothered her. But this time it was coming from her, from her skin, her breath. I am decomposing, I can feel myself decomposing, she would say as I wiped the sweat off her brow with a towel. I could feel her dying sweat sticking to me, the stench penetrating my hair, following me everywhere. Later I learned how to put a few drops of plain vinegar in the rinse water after shampooing my hair to completely banish it. Recalling that now, I have been rinsing my hair with vinegar water for the past three nights, but I can still smell the pervasive odour of death in this apartment. It is attenuated, so faint that only I can perceive it, but it will not leave me, not yet.

In the days that remain before my return to Warsaw, apart from cleaning the apartment I still have to take out the garbage, leave the bottles outside – there is always somebody who will take them back to the store for five cents apiece – pay the rest of the bills and have the gas disconnected. The new tenant in this second-floor apartment on St Mark's Place in the East Village will have nothing but words of praise for my diligent housekeeping. Almost all outgoing tenants leave behind at least some grime, a thin film of grease on the stove, or at the very least a brown ring at the bottom of the toilet bowl. But I wanted to eradicate all traces of me and José in the apartment. As if a drop of strong acid had fallen on a greasy stain and dissolved it.

Among other things, before leaving I had to decide what to do with the two black-and-white enlarged photographs of José. I hesitated to destroy them, because they were all I had left of my lover. I do not want to take anything with me to Warsaw that might remind me of him, not the smallest memento, and least of all a photograph. His two portraits hung on the wall of the deserted bedroom. Outside the December sun shone brightly that afternoon, its light tracing a hazy rectangle on the floor. Suddenly the room assumed an unreal, portentous appearance, as if a mysterious light illuminated it from within. I had closed the bedroom door, for no obvious reason. I was alone in the apartment. It was probably a subconscious precaution, as though if the door were left even slightly ajar, something might slip out. A secret which had to stay sealed in this room forever.

I leaned on the windowsill of a room I would soon be leaving, a room where the most important thing in my life had happened. I was alone with his photographs. How could José ever have lived surrounded by them and not been bothered by constantly running into his own face? The portraits had been my idea, reflections of my own need to have him always present, in whatever way possible. I remember thinking, when putting them up, that the photographs would be my only souvenir of him. Looking at these two remaining photographs, I felt like laughing at my own naïveté in believing that such images could ever be important mementos of our relationship. How could I ever have believed, even briefly, that José would return to Brazil?

I was about to burn them when I stopped. Something kept me from doing it. I recognized the move of his hands, the folds in his trousers, the dirty white sneakers. My inner picture of José overlapped with that of the photograph, and suddenly it was as if he had come alive. It hurt, although I knew that both pain and extreme loneliness were merely the unimportant consequences of my new situation. What was important was the peace, the inner serenity felt by someone who had finally achieved her goal. He was already inside me, I simply had not yet had time to get used to his presence.

The full-length photograph of him standing by the playground fence in front of the basketball court at West Fourth Street was the last one I had taken, and the other portrait was one of the first, right after he had moved in with me. Yet, looking at them, it was the portrait that seemed like the last visual image I had left of him. Those familiar light speckles in his eyes as he looked out of this same window while I snapped him with my idiot box of a camera, using a roll of black-and-white film left over from Poland. And then those same speckles in his eyes three months later, as he lay in bed. In the photograph I thought I detected a trace of fatigue in the circles under his eyes after three sleepless nights in his dormitory room. We had not left his room for three days and three nights, and then we had come here and I had photographed him, already utterly captivated by his face, by his body.

Only the firm line of his upper lip spoiled the relaxed expression of his face. As if etched with a knife, that line, at first glance, gave his face an expression of cruelty and lustfulness, and it made me tremble. It was the same the first time I ever saw him. José's strange ability to disturb the

7

balance of my being, even in a photograph, to make me react physically, was what stopped me from destroying it immediately. That and the fact that it was clear in the photograph that he was still not entirely aware of what had happened to him. Because, when that picture was taken, three months ago, José thought his life was an integral whole and that he was still in control of it.

In the other picture he was wearing dark glasses and his face was veiled and silent. His right hand, holding a cigarette, was half raised in what looked like a nervous, defensive gesture. The daylight streamed in from every side – from the edges of the photograph, from the whiteness of the crushed carton, from the billboard in the distance. That encroaching light of the city moved in on him, swathed him, enveloped him and was absorbed into his skin. Although hidden behind dark glasses, his face was caught in a moment of extreme vulnerability and immortalized by the camera.

That shot was taken no more than three weeks ago, and even though I can pinpoint the time, it is of absolutely no relevance to the inner scheme of things. What is important is the picture of that moment that is imprinted on my mind. Those last few days I carried a camera with me everywhere, as if, anticipating our separation, I did not dare rely on my own memory. Then, three weeks ago, when the end was not only quite certain but also in part planned, I still could not shake off the desire to photograph him. Even then, though, I knew that I would later destroy all these images. They were too shallow and paltry to keep as mementos.

It was a milky day, as if coated in cream. I remember we had come out of the West Fourth Street subway station. The stairs reeked of urine and the iron railing was slippery with rain. I slipped and grabbed the hem of his leather jacket. I carried the touch of leather in my hand all the way up to the top of the stairs. To the left were a wire fence and high, graffiti-covered dark brick walls. Behind José's shoulders, two solid slabs of wall joined to form a right angle. High, high above hung a curdled patch of sky. He walked towards me slowly, one hand in the pocket of his short black jacket, and the other raising a cigarette to his lips. As I clicked the camera, I wished I had a powerful weapon in my hand, a pistol, perhaps a knife, something with which I could at any moment sever all the threads connecting him to life, to this place, to me. And then swallow that still living piece of reality. Keep it for myself, forever. He walked over to me, kissed my face without saying a word and then suddenly turned his eyes away.

I did not realize until I had destroyed all my photographs of him that for me the picture-taking had been a kind of magic, reflecting the desire for total possession, for gaining power over him. As I looked at the photographs, I thought of how José should have been in São Paulo now, walking the streets somewhere near his house, weighed down by the crushing density of the first few days of our separation, which dropped off his back one by one, like rocks. The photographs were so charged with motion that he looked as if he were about to step out of the frame. I had taken a few steps around the room before I realized that the energy in these photographs had shifted; it was now inside me, I was actually lending it my own body. It was not just me walking, but him as well. This feeling of twoness caught me unprepared.

But I know I will have to get used to it, to this feeling of him coming alive inside me, to the power I feel he has over me as a result.

I have no idea why, but as I was walking around the room, I wondered how an outsider would see all this. And then I felt a rush of hatred which surprised me. It was not directed at anyone in particular. I simply felt a kind of abstract, suffocating hatred because I suspected that no one else could understand the way my lover and I had stayed bonded to each other, the way our beings had permeated each other and intermixed, the way we had finally become one. And then the feeling vanished as suddenly as it had appeared.

The light in the room changed. The day was slowly starting to yellow, giving the photographs a sepia colour, the colour of sorrow. I knew that this was the right moment to destroy them. As I tore them up, the fragility of the paper surprised me. I burned them piece by piece over the sink, the curls of black ash slowly disappearing down the drain.

It was hard to clean the whole apartment, but it was even harder to wipe it clean of our presence. I felt as if I were peeling off a thin, transparent foil which had invisible signs of our former life glued on to it. I was peeling it off the walls, the floors, the tiles. Luckily, only a few of José's things remained, packed in a carrier bag: an address book, documents, spiral-bound writing pads with research notes for his book, a small English–Portuguese dictionary, the keys to his apartment and car in São Paulo. It was not hard for me to get rid of these things. I hesitated only over José's notes. For all my resolve, after his death I found it hard to part with absolutely everything. José's notes on cannibalism, for instance, were the key to understanding our relationship and everything that had happened between us. Which is why I decided to hold on to them, just temporarily, so that once I got home to Warsaw, I could read at least those parts written in English. I got rid of everything else. I left some of his books at the Forty-Second Street branch of the Public Library (they check your bags only when you leave, not upon entering – it never occurred to them that someone might visit the library in order to leave books inside) and the rest I left in a nearby second-hand bookstore. Of course, I was careful not to be seen. Who gives books away in this day and age? I suppose I could have paid someone a commission to sell them for me, but then I would have had to have left an address. The clothes were easy: I gave them to the homeless. I sold two suitcases at the flea market around the corner, along with the green Hubertus coat. The only things I regretted disposing of were the toys José had bought for his son, a battery-operated white bunny and a rubber puppy. The rest were odds and ends: a purple lighter of the cheapest variety; an unfinished box of Gitanes; a cassette of Brazilian music; Clarice Inspector's book *Uma aprendizagem ou o livro doz prazeres*, which I found thrust in among the newspapers in the kitchen; his grey pullover. He had been wearing it that last evening. I had been tempted to keep it, mostly because of the smell. But I didn't. Knowing that I would be tempted, I had decided in advance that all this unnecessary para-phernalia, all these clothes, papers, plastic objects, should be disposed of as soon as possible. It is funny how all the evidence of a life together ultimately comes down to the crumbling fragments of a large fresco of faded colours. As if any of these oddments could bring back the softness of his palms, his freckled back, his upper arm with its mole, his stringy wet hair after a shower or his face as he leaned over me. I did not dare be sentimental or unnecessarily self-indulgent; I had no reason to be tearful. But I realized that only after I left New York would I be able to feel, purely and utterly, this union with my internalized, fully attained love.

11

The other day on Park Avenue, I noticed two people our age with a child. There was something touching about how they bent over the baby carriage and how their faces assumed the same worried expression. So, I thought, it is possible to live like that. To walk down the street on a holiday afternoon, enter a restaurant, hold the child in one's lap and order a beer. When they sat down the man looked out, past the woman's face, but keeping it within his range of vision. It takes so much effort to survive, a man has so little time to relax, his gaze told me. And when he finally does have the time to stroll through the park, sit down and order a drink or visit a friend, that must never be the moment when he thinks how his life is as empty as a dead shell. Perhaps he can allow himself a fleeting awareness of this feeling, which will suddenly blow away like the wind. But nothing more than that. And even that should be suppressed, forgotten as soon as possible, washed down with yet another glass to get him through the day.

Yesterday, Christmas Eve, the sky was pale blue, like the finest blue silk. As I was cleaning up around the house, I heard a man shout something outside, down in the street, and then a car door slamming. The street was quiet otherwise, dreamy, like a Sunday afternoon. Again I had a strong sensation of José's presence.

It was late morning in São Paulo at that moment. If he were there José might be playing with his son on the beach, trickling the fine, dry sand on the child's feet. Felipe would wriggle his little toes and laugh. He was nine months old. José would cover the boy's head with a white cotton cap to protect him against the sun, even though in Brazil it was only the beginning of summer. Then he would glance at his watch. Time to put the child down for a sleep. I imagined him picking up the boy, brushing the grains of sand off his little body and walking toward the small wooden beach house. He would feel the child's warmth and smell his sweat as the boy laid his head on his father's shoulder and fell asleep. José would enter the house and put the child down in his crib. He would sit in the darkened room for a while, listening to the child breathe. The little boy's mother would not be back from town until late afternoon – she had gone to buy presents for the friends who would be coming round later. That evening, dressed in a white shirt and trousers, José would drink whisky as the sweat trickled down his back. Leaning against the wall, taking large swigs of his drink, he would answer questions about his stay in New York with a quick yes or no. To a backdrop of loud toasting, taking fresh gulps which scorched the throat, he would suppress the vague unease he felt. I will make the effort, I have to make the effort to live. This is my real life. José would be aware that his life was an extremely delicate paper construction which could be destroyed instantaneously by the merest thoughtless touch.

In the past three days I have noticed that my body has gradually become increasingly hard, as if my skin were turning into metal armour. When I rub my hands, it feels as if the dry rustle of skin is coming from somewhere far away. On the subway to the Bronx, carrying one of the big, tightly tied garbage bags which I had put in a dark blue New Man sports bag, I stared so hard at the man sitting across from me that he had to look away.

Looking at him, I thought of how José had lost nothing.

I shall have to get used to this new presence of his which suddenly seizes me like a fit. Having disposed of yet another 'package' – I left it in the garbage bin of a fish restaurant near the East River – I sat down in a small French bakery on East Fourth Street. We had gone there together once. I remembered the three round stone-topped tables the colour of freshly sliced chicken. I ordered a cappuccino. As soon as I took my first sip I felt the anxiety I now recognized as longing, or rather anticipation. As if, by merely turning my head, I would see José sitting in his coat and scarf – he was constantly cold in New York – gazing at the sidewalk across the street. Perhaps at the girl with the sturdy thighs hurrying across the intersection. Then I would see him absently take a sip from his paper cup and put it down on the table, revolted by the taste of the wax on his lips. Shit, I would hear him say in an accusing voice, his eyes searching my face for confirmation of his betrayal by the coffee cup. Or by the cold. Or by the city. The smell of freshly baked rolls wafted in through the open door behind the counter. It was a wet day, but it had stopped raining before I came in. A woman carrying a huge bouquet of white chrysanthemums stopped in front of the shop window. Her face was wreathed in a smile, as if she had found what she had been looking for. I wondered whether José had noticed her smile, as again he lifted the paper cup to his lips, but at that moment I realized that he was not there, that there really was no José; that he did not exist. That he was not next to me as I sat there thinking, observing the street, while the girl in the short skirt and the woman with the chrysanthemums passed by. It was me sipping the cappuccino, me tasting the wax paper on my lips, but now these lips were both mine and his, as was the sense of betrayal, of feeling lost, which was now nestling in my soul. I felt like a lined coat, as if José's skin lay just inside my own.

As I was putting José's notes away in my suitcase, a photograph of the two of us, taken in one of those automatic booths, fell out. It was a very small picture, silly really, but

I stopped to look at it because it was the only picture of the two of us together. What had brought this strange, roughly attractive man from Brazil and this seemingly frail blonde woman from Poland to this photo booth at Penn Station in the winter of that year? What was the force that had held them together twenty-four hours of each of the seventy-six days they had spent together in this city? And what was the force that had separated them? Could they even be said to have been separated simply because one of them was now dead?

I woke up the other day thinking I was a murderer, but the sounds of the house emerging from its slumber managed to drive the thought away, if only for a while. The three-storey building awoke slowly, like an old lady. First you could hear the squeak of the unoiled door – I wonder how long it has been squeaking like that, and how much longer it will go on doing so? – and Madam Victoria taking her little dog, an old Maltese called Misha, out for a walk. I heard the scratch of its paws on the landing outside my front door. Mack, who sang in a choir, began his morning voice exercises in the bathroom, and at that same moment the actress (or more precisely, waitress) in the apartment above me put on her aerobic exercise tape. The sounds were soothing; they gave me a feeling of safety, a special kind of safety. As though I was protected by the presence of these people, by their very existence and their daily repetition of the same actions, like a ritual. Every day was the same as the day before, as the day I had arrived in New York, the day José had moved in with me and the day he had disappeared. Every morning the man did his voice exercises, the little dog went for its walk, the ceiling shook from the unrelenting jumping of the anorexic waitress and the smell of real Italian espresso coffee wafted up from the ground-floor apartment. Mine was the only apartment in the building being rented out – illegally. They call it sub-letting here. The leaseholder, Susan, a political scientist at NYU, was away in Europe on a study trip. There had been quite a turnover of subletters, mostly foreign scholarship students from the university.

Perhaps the word 'murderer' had been evoked by sounds which had suddenly become too loud, as though echoing through an empty apartment. Nothing moved in this apartment: I heard not a single sound except for the beating of my own heart. That emptiness, that stillness, that immured dead silence. Solitude covered me like a thin blanket of ice, and I wriggled deeper into my bed. There was still so much to do, to tidy up, put in order, clean, I thought despondently. For three solid days now I had been flopping into bed and falling asleep instanta-neously. In the morning I would be wrenched from a deep sleep by the ringing of the alarm clock.

But that morning, I woke up in the empty apartment with the word 'murderer', like a brick tossed in through the window while I was asleep.

It did not make me think I really was a murderer, but for the first time I realized that this was how people might see me. Perhaps it was not until that morning that I could look at my situation from the outside. If somebody were to con-front me right now with the facts of the last three days of my life, that is how it would look, as if I had coldbloodedly, and with premeditation, killed, in fact smothered, my lover José with a pillow while he was asleep, having first plied him with drink and slipped him a large quantity of sleeping pills. That had been on Tuesday evening. Over the days that followed I had disposed not only of his things, but also of his remains, cleaned up the apartment and got ready to leave. On the surface, that is what I did. I took his life, I killed him – although the very word makes me sick, as indeed does the thought of any kind of violence. But that is not at all what this is about: it is about the possibility of prolonging life, about a way of allowing us to stay together. José's death was merely a necessary detail, an unavoidable step towards achieving union; a means, not an end. Had there been any other way, any other solution to the relationship in which we found ourselves, to that serpentine intertwining of our beings, none of this would have happened. That is why I am not sorry that he had to die. Generally speaking, the word grief, like the word death, like so many other words I could use here, is completely meaningless. None of these words embrace or describe anything, because as categories they simply do not apply to this particular case. Grief is an entirely human category, and the reason for his death totally transcends that.

II

The beginning was very simple and, as always, pure chance was at the heart of it. Or a series of chance happenings which ultimately became fate. I first saw José at the main branch of the New York Public Library on the corner of Fifth Avenue and Forty-Second Street. It was already early October, but the day was hot and I found the reading room refreshingly cool. As soon as I walked in I immediately lost that sense of insecurity that Eastern Europeans carry with them like baggage whenever they step into a system they are not used to. Here everything looked familiar, except for the computerized catalogue system, but I soon mastered that as well. The suffused light from outside, the dark, wood-panelled walls, the old bronze lamps on the long tables and the soft uneven sound of turning pages pleasantly rustling between the fingers. And then something I relished in advance: the smell of old cloth- and leather-bound books, their fragile paper and the invisible layers of dust which, after leafing through the pages, sticks to my fingers as I open some old catalogue.

It was the book that first caught my eye. Bound in black cloth, it was lying on top of a stack of books on the other side of the table. All I saw, embossed in gold letters on the

spine, was its title: *Divine Hunger*. I don't know why I did it –
perhaps because of the beautiful letters which leaped out
at me from their dark setting, or the strange title, or the
particular moment I noticed the book – but I reached out
and pulled it to my side of the table without even looking
at the person sitting opposite me. I now think that that
must have been the first chance happening which led to all
the others. I suppose I expected it to be a book of poetry,
maybe because in my hands I was already holding a study
of metaphysical poets. According to the contents page,
however, this was some sort of specialized anthropological
study of cannibalism by a Peggy R. Sanday, published by
Cambridge University Press, with classifications and tables
of the geographic distribution of exo-cannibalism and
endo-cannibalism. At the time, nothing in the world could
have interested me less than a study of cannibalism. I
closed the book and put it back, but the title still intrigued
me. *Divine Hunger*. God and hunger. I remember repeating
to myself those two words, so resonant on my tongue, and
deciding that I should use them in a poem. It did cross my
mind that the idea that cannibalism brought man closer to
the divine was not so strange, but I did not dwell on it.
From that moment on, however, these three notions were
firmly connected in my subconscious by the thin, steely
thread of language.

The man across the way, to whom the book obviously
belonged, was writing something in his spiral-bound notebook, his head bowed, looking as if he had not even
noticed that I had taken the book from under his nose
not a minute earlier. He had a strange way of turning the
pages of his notebook, with his fingertips raised. It was as if
he were taking care not to let them touch the paper
because it would be painful for him. Later, standing on

the wide white front steps of the building, unable to decide which way to go – downtown toward the university in the Village or uptown, in the direction of the nearest Barnes & Noble bookstore – my skin still feeling the coolness and protection of the reading room, I caught sight again of the title of the book and the slightly raised fingertips. The man from across the table was now standing next to me, offering me the book. 'Take a better look if it interests you,' he said. 'I can wait.' I took the book, although I was not really interested in it any more. That, perhaps, was the second, decisive chance happening. Because, though we could not have known it at the time, our future was contained in those two simple gestures of accepted communication, in his offering the book and in my taking it.

As soon as he opened his mouth I knew he was a foreigner. I had already learned how to recognize nuances in English pronunciation. That comes automatically when you are a foreigner yourself, when you are focused on one thing only, on the fear of not understanding or not being understood and, therefore, of missing something important. Of not catching every word, sound and intonation, that fine web of barely detectable shades which denote a joke or irony, for instance. The worst are those ordinary phrases meant to facilitate communication, but whose meaning it takes foreigners a long time to understand. I had studied English language and literature and was familiar with it, but since coming here I had realized that there was a major difference between what was spoken and what was written, between looking at the text as a written language and listening to a living language. I was afraid of that, I am still afraid of the meaning escaping me, as if this foreign language and this foreign city are an ocean which will swallow me up sooner or later.

'You must be a foreigner, too,' I said. The word had a magic effect, suddenly dispelling the uncomfortable tension that grips you when you are addressed by a complete stranger. We were both foreigners, and that immediately bonded us. Paradoxically, the fact that we were not each speaking our own language made it easier, rather than more difficult, to strike up a conversation. Even though we both made a conscious and careful effort to express ourselves clearly, using a foreign language was liberating. It allowed us to talk rapidly and impulsively, without weighing every word for its inevitable inadequacy. The very word 'foreigner' is redolent of common experience: your first arrival in New York, the young man who takes your suitcase and puts it in the taxi outside the terminal building, charging five dollars for the service; the people who promise to help you find an apartment and then 'forget'; the coins you have to learn to tell apart; the noise, the wailing sirens, the constant tension in the streets – this is where they mug, rob and kill, to quote our papers. And all the time the constant effort to leave the opposite impression: that you are not a foreigner, that you know your way around the subway, the streets and the strange customs of this frenzied city. Then comes the ponderous desire to forget the grant and the doctorate and the wondrous opulence of the department stores, a feeling that grips you after a week, just when you start to relax, when you already have a sure handle on the city, on your lecture schedule at the university; when you are getting to know the shops, restaurants and movie theatres in your neighbourhood. That desire to return to the safety, the familiarity of your shabby everyday life, which from here looks like a refuge slipping farther and farther away.

The man said his name was José. What a literary name,

I laughed, like a character from a picaresque novel. He laughed too, and the way his face lit up made him look interesting, although until that moment I had not been aware of any desire to see him again. 'I wish it were,' he said, 'but it's a very common name in Brazil.' Then he told me that he had written several anthropological books and one semi-successful novel. I have to say I liked the way he classified his own work, although I was not sure that it wasn't false modesty. He also said that he lectured at the university, because who could possibly earn a living writing in such a poor country as Brazil? He had recently received a three-month grant to write a book about the 1972 plane crash in the Andes – the famous case of the young Uruguayan rugby players who survived for seventy days in the mountains by eating human flesh. He was not interested in the case itself – enough had been written about that already – he was interested in a particular aspect of it, the subsequent public debate on cannibalism and the Catholic Church. José offered this more by way of an explanation for the book he was holding, whose title had caught my eye, rather than as a serious attempt to define the problem for me.

'And you? Do you write too?' he asked.

I don't know what made him ask me that, or why I said, 'No . . . actually, yes.'

'Yes, and no?' he asked in smiling disbelief. 'How's that?'

'Yes and no,' I asserted. 'I'm writing my doctoral thesis.' I did not mention the poetry. Anyway, I could not lay claim to even semi-success. But the real reason was that it was hard for me to admit to a stranger that I wrote poetry. I was always afraid that a pronouncement like that might startle people, as if I had a visible physical defect or a serious disease. Essays, novels, a doctoral thesis, it all sounded so serious and sensible, somehow, something one might even be able to make some sort of living from. Poetry was different. I remember having this feeling even then, when answering his question, that my job at the university, my metaphysical poets, my one published and two unpublished collections of poems, my life thus far, were part of the past, something which was receding, leaving room for the unknown yet to come. Perhaps it was simply a question of language, although it does not seem so now. The fact remains that I talked about my life in Poland in the past tense. As if it was not about me, I thought, the taste of my words still fresh in my mouth.

José bought Italian ices at the stand on the corner. We ate and laughed at the way he poked a hole in the middle of the pinkish scoop with his tongue, and I licked my pistachio into the shape of a cone. We sat next to each other on the steps, our shoulders almost touching, as if eating together had created yet another bond between us, yet another possibility for understanding. Judging this as the threshold of intimacy, which we had already crossed, José asked for my telephone number. I thought he should have realized by then that he could find me at this same library almost every day. His question seemed too predictable, too stereotypical. I looked at him carefully. Actually, I dared take a closer look at him only once I was virtually certain that I would never see him again. He had a long, narrow face, thick eyebrows and dark eyes. Handsome, I thought. Smooth, somehow; sleek, elusively handsome, like a model in a fashion magazine. But his face would have looked almost empty, like a mask of unreal beauty, had it not been for the full, sensual lips which gave it an expression of hardness, determination, perhaps even cruelty. I realized then that it was because of them, because of those lips, that I had reached out for the book a second time, that I had talked, smiled, eaten ice cream. I closed my eyes and briefly imagined his lips, cold and wet from the ice cream, sliding down my belly, and the image fired such desire inside me that it was as if my body had already surrendered to his touch, as if that touch had become inevitable. Still, I did not give him my phone number or any additional explanation.

When he left I felt like a child who has found something precious and lost it.

Entering the library a few days later, instead of going up to the third floor, I walked straight on. I wondered why I had not noticed this exhibition before and how often I had already passed the door which said: From Portugal to Brazil: The Age of Atlantic Discovery. I went inside only because of that one word, because of a sensitivity to that word, to its sound, to the way José had pronounced it. *Braziu*, that is how it is pronounced, he had said. The exhibition room was almost empty and the small group of people gathered around the museum guide, a tall grey-haired woman, moved slowly from one exhibit to the next. 'The astrolabe dates from the beginning of the sixteenth century and is one of the oldest in the world. It will be a long time before you get another chance to see something as old as this,' said the guide in too loud a voice, as if addressing a class of restless schoolchildren instead of a group of adults. She looked around to check the impression she had created and seemed taken aback. It must have been only then that she noticed that the people she was addressing were mostly dark-skinned, that they were clearly foreigners, and that she had been accidentally put into a situation where, quite inappropriately, she was telling them about what was probably their own history. 'Please correct me if I make a mistake,' she said in a quieter voice. But no one uttered a word. There was something strange about this scene, about the people listening to her attentively, and then quietly commenting to each other in Portuguese. Perhaps it was pure coincidence that this particular batch of visitors was obviously South American. They looked like recent arrivals, possibly tourists or perhaps immigrants. They had come, probably drawn by the word 'Brazil' which, inscribed in yellow, in the colour of the sun and gold, fluttered on the blue flag outside the library. The woman fell silent for a moment. Perhaps she was thinking about this small group of people whose shoes still carried the dust of the country drawn on the old maps they had just been examining. They had come from another world, one she knew absolutely nothing about, and she realized that she should be quiet and not say another word. But she had to go on talking about the things she knew simply from the catalogue, which any visitor could buy for nine dollars a throw. In the final analysis, that was what she was paid for.

The group stopped in front of a 1505 woodcut by Johann Froschauer depicting Brazilian Indians eating a dismembered human body: one man was eating a severed arm, pieces of the torso were strewn on the ground, a body was hanging from the roof of a hut, and the children, looking as if they had overeaten, were dragging along what remained of the human entrails. 'I don't show this picture when there are children in the group,' said the woman. A man in the group turned his head away, as if he personally had been responsible for the massacre.

We moved on to a seventeenth-century painting of maritime routes. The woman recited a badly memorized text about the long voyages of Portuguese seafarers who had only the stars to guide them. I thought of José, and of how maybe five hundred years ago one of his ancestors had embarked on a mad adventure, voyaging into the unknown, his hunger and unreliable hand-drawn maps taking him south of *terra nova*, toward the region which was later to become Puerto Sicuro, Guanabara, El Brasil – and which the French called the French Antarctic. I imagined the loneliness of those seafarers and the rolling of the dark, leaden sea on the horizon. Day after day, night after night. For months, until they stopped measuring time. The sky would sometimes drop so low over the ship that it looked as if it would crush it. Once a man found himself on a ship heading across the Atlantic, there was no going back, no escape. He had to keep sailing toward the unknown, his eyes riveted to the stars. Every man was alone on this voyage, enclosed in his body as if in a fragile shell. It must have been cold on those small wooden sailing vessels in the middle of the ocean, cold from the wind and the loneliness. People must have jumped into the sea sometimes, simply unable to take it any more. They must have felt they would never set eyes on land again. But there on the hazy green coastline which one morning finally surfaced from the sea's mist, stood some people, and one of them might later have become another ancestor of José's.

Exhibited in a glass case was a copy of Pero Vaz de Caminho's letter to King Manuel, written on 1 May 1500. 'They were dark and completely naked, with nothing to cover their shame. They all moved boldly toward the ship and Nicolau Coelho signalled them to lay their bows down on the ground, and they obeyed him. He could not exchange a single word with them, or understand them.' The killing by both sides, the attempts at extermination, went on for a long time, but in the end they did intermix. I wondered whether José felt these two conflicting currents flowing and clashing inside him, like two streams of blood.

As I walked around the exhibition, I became increasingly aware that these pictures and words were reminding me too much of someone I had seen only once, and even then only for half an hour.

Suddenly, there was a clearly recognizable presence. I did not see him, I simply felt his closeness behind me. We almost touched, the warmth of his body already mingling with mine. The group moved on to the large oil painting, *The Presentation,* but we remained where we were, standing between the model of the sailing ship and Froschauer's print, where our eyes met. It could not have been anyone else. My skin recognized him as if we had already exchanged touches. We stood there motionless, as if the slightest movement could have unforeseeable consequences. Time passed. I heard it in the shuffling of shoes as the visitors walked around the exhibition.

There was still a gap between us, an invisible space, like an obstacle which would not let us get completely close. I sensed a wisp of my own hesitance in turning around, more in the way I was breathing, shifting my balance from one foot to the other. I thought how at that moment, before we touched, everything was still possible. Non-recognition. A change of mind. Escape.

I was still free. For a brief time yet his presence would not mean anything to me. It could be someone else standing there behind me. I could turn around and look into the face of a complete stranger who was standing too close. Perhaps I would push him away. He would slip, fall and hit his head against the smooth stone floor. There would be the echoing thud of his fall, like that of a clay dish. I would bend down and see a dark fracture on his brow, just a thin line. And just as I began to think that it was nothing, blood would start to seep out of the crack.

I stood there stock still, relishing this moment of secret anticipation, watching the possibility of my retreat fade away, like the voice of the guide, who was now talking about the model of the ship. When I turned around, his eyes plunged eagerly into mine. I had an almost physical reaction to the keenness of recognition, as if that very instant I had taken a pair of scissors and cut José out of the scene. The background suddenly shrank away, fixed like a lifeless painting on the wall. José said something, but I was not listening. There was no need to explain the coincidence.

I knew it was just a matter of time before I would sleep with him. The signs were easy to read, in the tension of the muscles, in the breathing, the surge of blood and warmth which congealed somewhere deep inside me. Mostly I knew it from the sudden, unexpected, sharp awareness of the body: I was returning to the body, to desire, to myself.

Perhaps we would have met anyway, since we both had grants for NYU. There were any number of occasions when we could have met, from interesting lectures to receptions at the various departments. We both probably avoided the latter. Later I realized that though José excused himself on the grounds of his poor English, in fact he was very shy and very busy. He had a pile of notes to make and only a three-month grant to cram it all in, with the possibility of perhaps extending it by an extra month. Such receptions, ostensibly the ideal environment in which to meet as many people as possible and feel less of a foreigner, had exactly the opposite effect on me: they depressed me. After these parties, where people ate crackers, cheese, grapes and raw vegetables dipped in some sort of greenish, spicy sauce, and drank wine out of plastic glasses, and where I was constantly exposed to superficial, dull-witted questions about the political situation in my country, I felt an even stronger urge to retreat to my apartment, slip into my bed, read poetry or listen to the cockroaches scuttling around the wooden floor. I had been lucky with my apartment. I had inherited it from a girl I knew who had returned to Warsaw and last semester had gone through the same rites of initiation into campus life that seemed to be reserved for foreign women. The thing is, Ana had told me, there is always some professor who thinks he will be a godsend, if only briefly, to a slightly lost female colleague from the exotic reaches of Eastern Europe, which is in vogue these days. She, of course, should be grateful that an American male, of an age which in other countries is already considered old, who exercises in the morning and jogs until his thin little wreath of grey hair flutters in the wind that blows in from the East River, wants to make her day by visiting her bed. She told me immediately that first on the list would be G.S., 'the greatest living American poet', as he was wont to introduce himself. I had been in New York less than a week when, at an English Department reception for graduate students, G.S. approached me with those very words, albeit spoken in a mildly self-deprecating tone. His lips were cold and damp on my hand. He invited me to breakfast. I accepted. I thought I was being polite. The next day, after breakfast, he leaned over to kiss me on the mouth, *droit de seigneur* of a full professor, I presume. I pulled back. He did not protest and I was grateful to him for that. He touched my forehead and cheek with his lips, as if my pulling back had automatically altered my status from that of a woman to that of a child who needed protection. From then on he addressed me as 'my child', which I found just as irritating, and told me how he had been to several of my father's concerts. The rest of the time he just sat there quietly, poised and pathetic. While he talked about Czeslaw Milosz, I watched the soggy crumbs of bread collect in the corners of his mouth. Every so often he would lick them away. I could barely restrain myself from wiping his mouth with the palm of my hand. I thought how old he was, how his body must have already taken on that smell of old age which nothing can camouflage, and which leaves its traces in bed, as if a sick man has been lying there. Sometimes old age exudes an aggressive, unbearable stench of death.

Patrick, on the other hand, smelled of the sea, and when I told him so he said that was because he came from Boston, and because for three years he had earned his living on a yacht smuggling in cocaine from South America. Patrick was a graduate student of Polish literature and was quite a good translator of poetry. Ana had instructed him to help me settle in. One evening, maybe a week after my arrival, I invited him over to dinner as a thank you – nothing special, *piroshka* stuffed with sweet cabbage. He brought a bottle of red wine. He told me about his Irish father and Polish mother, about his eight sisters and brothers, and about how he had been unable to go to university until he had earned the money to pay for his studies. We sat in the living room, I on the couch, he in the armchair facing me. At one point he stood up, walked across the room and, as if he had been thinking about nothing else the entire time, he knelt down and took my leg in his hands. I was wearing black button-up high-heeled shoes, the old-fashioned kind. He looked youthful kneeling there at my feet, with his slate-blue eyes and red hair. While he was still in the armchair, I had recognized in the way he sprawled his legs out in front of him that insolence which comes with the body's instant readiness for sex. I noticed it immediately, just as I had noticed how his eyes kept darting to my shoes, to my black net stockings between the shoe and the hem of my skirt. His glance slid under my skirt like fingers, and to him I was naked before he had even begun to unbutton my shoe, which he held in his hand as he looked me in the eye. He kissed me slowly, the length of my leg, his tongue searching for the little holes in the net stockings. Then he lay on the floor and pulled me down on top of him. As I sat on him, my knees hugging his naked, muscular body, I thought that this was exactly the kind of lover I wanted, a young unknown man who could read my unspoken desire from the kind of shoes and stockings I wore, from my perfume, from my posture. A lover who would appear on Friday evening, leave on Sunday around noon and disappear for the rest of the week.

And for a short time that is exactly what he was. Patrick came on Fridays and helped me translate my poetry into English. He would bring red wine. I thought he was a good, confident lover. I was sure I knew the needs of my own body.

It's different for visiting academics, José told me later. Seventeen-year-old girls knock at the door of your room at night, and in the morning are sitting in class with traces of love bites still fresh on their necks. When I met him, I saw such traces on José's own neck, but it did not matter. What mattered was what drew me to him, although I still hesitate to define it. I only know that it was a case of being infected with his body and of my desire to possess him totally.

The first thing I packed away when I started cleaning the bathroom two days ago was my diaphragm. I did not use it with José, except for that last week when I knew that the end was near and I could no longer leave anything to chance. As I held the smooth little blue box in my hand, like a small sapphire coffin, I thought of that feeling of dissolving, of stripping off layers of each other's body. That was the only instrument we had, our only instrument of understanding, the language of the body which comes behind, in front of, beside the words, beside speech, which soon became insufficient for our needs. The body compensated for our lack of language, that something which had been eluding us from the very beginning.

Only the body gave me a direct route to him, to his dark inner side.

After we met at the exhibition we went straight to José's room. The university accommodation was only a few blocks away from my apartment so it seemed as though we both just happened to be taking the same train in the same direction. I watched him lean against the wall in the churning belly of the subway, wearing his white wrinkled shirt and white trousers, looking so quiet, so relaxed. Just as I had learned to decode voices – tones, volume, accents, hidden layers of meaning – so I was learning to read faces, and carefully to observe expressions: the focused gaze, the little wrinkles on his brow betraying thought, the eyebrows, the cock of the head, the rhythm of the pulse beating in the vein at his temple. The train was running late; José reached for a cigarette. In the movement of his hand I recognized the same tension, impatience and tautness I felt myself. Neither of us took a step back or made an unnecessary move, or asked the other where we were going. We behaved as if we were both performing a task with absolute assurance, automatically, almost; unquestioningly, because it came from a higher power. When he took my hand at the subway exit, I felt as if he had been standing there for a long time, waiting. The palm of his hand was as soft as a child's. The unexpected tenderness, something about that palm which seemed so vulnerable, filled me at once with sadness. As we walked down the street, our step quickening, I could not help thinking: I shall sleep with him now and then perhaps a few times more. Then he will leave, or I will leave, it does not matter which. 'Let's stay friends,' he will say. The force leading us blindly to bed will soon be exhausted, spent. We shall exchange a few letters, they will get shorter and shorter, and, of course, there will be the obligatory Christmas and New Year cards. He will invite me to visit him over the summer (I can stay with his best friend), but I will not answer. Anyway, nothing should be expected of such chance encounters except naked, slippery passion which leaves no scars. We walked in silence as though our haste had taken away our power of speech. But when at last we entered his room and I undid the top button of my dress, I was no longer so sure that things would quite turn out that way.

If I shut my eyes I can still reconstruct the scene as if I were both in it and outside it – as if it happened to me and to somebody else at the same time. He closes the door of the room and leans against it. The door is now doubly closed. There is not a sound from outside, as if the room's walls are covered in velvet and soundproof. I see myself standing in the middle of the room, dappled with afternoon light. I am wearing only a light dress which I can hardly feel on me. The fabric is thin and his gaze easily penetrates it, circles my breasts, brushes my stomach and hips. Men know that it is a dress to be whisked off in a sweep of the arm; it is made for them to whisk off. But that is not what he does. He stands there watching my fingers open my dress, watching them open me. He knows he can stand it no longer, yet still he does not move away from the door, still he waits, waits for me to surrender to him completely, and to do it alone. I see myself finally whisking off the dress myself, standing there naked, defenceless. He draws the curtains and in the semi-darkness and silence kisses me very slowly, solemnly.

His lips taste of peaches.

I remember that first kiss, that feeling of rapidly shrinking: suddenly I am so small that I am immersed in him, I drown in his moist throat. All of me is in his mouth, like a morsel of food. He takes me into himself and swallows and as I sink into the warm darkness I feel myself disappearing inside him. I dissolve, and he absorbs me as if we shall never part again.

I enter a dark chamber where nothing but the senses exist.

I woke up in the middle of the night. I was lying on my side; he was curled around me like ivy. I remember thinking how crazy it was to surrender myself to a total stranger like that. What exactly had happened? Why had I not gone into the bathroom and put in my diaphragm? What degree of irrationality was this? Did I have some unknown overpowering desire for his love, a desire which made me stay in the room with him and not want to interrupt the touch, the warmth flowing from one body to the other?

Just when I had learned that life was predictable, just when I had finally given up waiting for something to change, this yearning for a true encounter had to surface. Suddenly, a perfectly chance meeting had destroyed the already thin protective membrane of my being, and a desperate, deep loneliness had risen to the surface. A refusal to reconcile myself to the life I was leading, to death, whose traces I already noticed on my face. Had I dared take a closer look in the mirror, I would have seen that I was covered in a rash of loneliness. Touching was no longer governed by youthful curiosity about the unknown. It became a way of drawing closer together, a defence against loneliness. The only important thing was to open up, to push aside all the obstacles standing in the way.

To be close as to the bone. To be close, as in death.

That night as we lay in his narrow bed breathing in unison, as if impressed on each other, both foreigners in a no man's land. I sensed that by morning these two bodies, these two isolated capsules, would create a separate world all of their own.

In the morning José brought warm black bread sprinkled with poppy seeds from the nearby Russian bakery, young cheese, pâté, butter, slices of watermelon, ice cream. We pounced voraciously on the food and then our hunger for food mixed with our hunger for each other. He fed me pieces of bread spread with pâté or butter. I licked the pâté off his fingers and the crumbles of cheese from the palm of his hand. When I had finished with the food, I moved on to eating his fingers and hands. At that moment, there was no difference between them. José rubbed the juice of the watermelon over my breasts, my shoulders, my arms. I melted a ball of butter between the palms of my hands and rubbed it over the smooth, long muscles of his legs, and then nibbled him, my sharp bites exciting him. There was no resistance from his body. He surrendered to my bites as if he found it impossible to fight off my insatiable hunger. At one point I imagined a roast joint and took a bite. I bit into his shoulder, and droplets of blood broke out on his skin. His blood was light pink, almost transparent. Slowly I let it stain his whole arm and then I licked the wound, like a dog. José fed me ice cream with a spoon and then took the ice cream from my mouth with his tongue. I know now that I should have recognized that first shared meal as a true desire to feed ourselves to each other and thus become one. Food was a part of our intimacy, our union, as important as touching itself.

We did not get out of bed for three days. We ate the left-overs. Outside day alternated with night, somebody knocked at the door. 'How can we suddenly be so hungry?' asked José, as if we had been starving until then. At the end of the third day our bodies were wounded and dirty. Showering together, for the first time I saw his body clearly, every vein under his skin, every muscle, bruise, bite, the shape of his shoulders and stomach – everything which had already been fed through my hands, my skin, my tongue. 'I don't know anything about you,' I said, although I knew my words were meaningless. My right to him had already been established, a right stronger than anything he could give me with a glimpse into his past.

That morning in the shower, I knew that everything that happened between us would have to be forever.

III

Perhaps things would have ended differently if José had not moved in with me. Our relationship would not have grown so quickly, so fatally, into a totally closed system which neither of us was capable of leaving, except at the cost of our lives. Every morning José had to shave the beard that grew overnight. He would stand in front of the bathroom mirror, feel his beard and lather it with slow, sleepy movements. He would wipe the foam off his lips with his index finger and light a cigarette. Every morning I watched him shave, brush his teeth, gargle, shower, pee and sit on the toilet reading the newspaper. We did not close any of the doors in the apartment. From the very beginning there were no doors in our relationship. This right to complete inspection, to complete insight into each other's lives, had been established the moment he moved into my apartment. José was not some visitor who knew he did not belong there, like Patrick. After the three days we had spent in his room, José immediately moved all his things in with me. We packed his suitcase together. Any other solution – meeting occasionally in town, going to the movies together and then to a restaurant – had been inconceivable from the start. What is more, the moment he entered my apartment on St Mark's Place I felt as if he had always been there. It seemed impossible that I had ever lived alone, that there had ever even been a time in my life when he had not existed. This was not something I decided, it was simply the nature of our relationship.

Sometimes I wish there had been some insurmountable technical obstacle to stop us from drowning in each other. We were like two desperate, surrounded terrorists, barricaded inside an isolated house and determined not to fall into the hands of the authorities alive. In the end they shoot each other in the mouth. This destructive energy, with which we isolated and absorbed each other, had emerged at our very first encounter, an energy on which we both fed and which could only grow and become increasingly insatiable.

José was married and had a son. At the end of the term he was due to return to his family in São Paulo. He mentioned it only incidentally, but anyway to me that part of his life clearly belonged to another world. Except for its information value, it had no real connection with what was happening between us in New York. When he told me, I thought how he said it was more important than what he said. He spoke in a flat voice, as if talking about what was showing at the movie theatre. Maybe that was deliberate, I do not know. I tried to imagine this wife of his, who, judging from what he said, could not have been much more than an amorphous lump of pulsating life, an amoeba who existed in some faraway, almost imaginary place. Still, I repeated his words in my mind several times, examining my inner sensitivity, like when a drop of lemon juice falls on your tongue and the mucous membrane contracts and produces more saliva. But the most I achieved was to imagine this wife as a spot on José's lung. Yes, exactly that, as an inherent benign disease with which it was quite possible to live.

He did not mention his son until later, when there was no danger that I might find him an obstacle, although I am not sure that it would have changed anything even if I had known earlier. Nevertheless, I flinched when José took out a photograph of him. I think José must have noticed a sudden wariness in my face at that moment. He did not mention his wife again, but he talked about Felipe as if there was no one else in São Paulo, just this little boy sitting naked in the sand and looking very much like his father. There was also the woman in the picture, the mother – Inês: I finally learned her name. She was leaning toward the child and her long brown hair screened her face from view. I was tempted to ask him for some more photographs, ones in which I could see her face, but I could not summon the strength for that. This is the only photograph I brought with me, José said, as if reading the unasked question. He talked about Felipe and how the boy had bitten him with his tiny new teeth just before José left. I laughed, as if Felipe were our child. José's shoulders relaxed. Then he stopped talking about him, or at least spoke of him less often as I expected. I had the feeling that he left the child outside, in front of the door, but always outside the scope of our relationship.

Naturally, however unimportant José's family was to me, it made me his mistress in the eyes of the outside world. Perhaps initially he had even hoped that by talking about his wife, he could mark the limits of my territory, fence off the space that did not belong to me – the future, for instance. But I did not accept these boundaries. He and I lived together in a small apartment in New York. So who was the wife, and who the mistress?

The second day after José moved in, I took some dirty sheets, towels, shirts, trousers and underwear, both his and mine, down to the washing machine in the basement. When the laundry was done and dried, José came down to the basement and carried it up to the apartment, already folded. On top were some of my panties, which had not washed properly (they were old and did not wash well). They bore the pale yellow traces of rinsed blood-stains. My hands trembled with excitement as I put them away in a drawer. As if José had hit me, or had come upon me unexpectedly and seen something forbidden. He did not notice my excitement. When I finally collected myself, I realized that José had acted quite automatically, quite unconsciously. He had done what he would have done with his wife's laundry in their São Paulo apartment. His simple gesture had completely equated me with her. That evening I made chicken soup, the kind we eat at home, with dumplings, lots of vegetables and white meat. I would not have made it for myself – it is a dish for bringing people around the table, for uniting people in misfortune or sickness, or for special occasions, if it does not form part of the family lunch. I did it to make him part of my own other reality, the one that was invisible to him. From the way he leaned over the plate, scooping up the soup with his spoon, completely immersed in his movements, I knew that he already belonged to me and me alone.

The longer we were together, the more I felt that our skin and flesh were melting, that our bodies were becoming extraneous.

José moved into my apartment in early October, but

soon it seemed as if it had been an October ten years ago. My perception of time past had become so compressed that I would get dizzy just trying to think back in a linear way. It is hard for me to remember now what we did in those three months. Nothing. We went to classes three times a week; the rest of the time we sat in the library. We tried to keep our outside schedules more or less unchanged, so as not to become completely immersed in our own world. Routine was vital; to an extent it was important to maintain this semblance of the outside world. Routine was the only thread that connected us with reality. The walls we erected against the outside kept growing. I could feel it by the way my hands would go numb when I sat across from him and watched him read. I was somehow strangely arrested, motionless, frozen in my observation of José. I would watch him hungrily, drinking in, breathing in his presence as he sat there with his open book, holding a pencil, turning a page, smoking. As if I wanted to encompass all of him with my eyes, to devour him with my eyes. Even now, when I know I will never see him again, when I am quite reconciled to it, the images which flash through my mind overshadow his words. At first I thought that the most important thing was to say everything, to articulate ourselves completely, to talk until even the smallest nuance of meaning was exhausted. Now his words circumvented me without a trace. Had I been able to reach him through words, had we been able to share them like a Christmas pudding which would have the same taste and same meaning for us both, then our relationship probably would have ended differently. But our common language was incomplete, like a net fabric on which we could barely rely, which barely connected us.

41

I discovered that José liked to talk about his dreams. It gave him more freedom to talk about himself, and thus to overcome the additional fear of doing so in a foreign language. But while he was telling me how he had dreamed he was sinking into red mud, I kept silent. I felt totally helpless, as if each word he uttered was sapping more and more of my strength. I knew he had a very definite picture in his mind at that moment, that he was talking about a shade of red he knew, about the red earth on his grandfather's property in Bahia. About the red silt of the river, the russet leaves of some primeval forest plants or water stained with the blood of a slaughtered lamb.

But that colour had existed in him before we met. That red mud he was talking about belonged to a world different from mine. I did not know that colour and would never see it as José did, stored as it was in his subconscious.

As he talked, I sat curled up in the armchair, trying to imagine the colours of his world, the light green at the edge of the jungle, its dark core; the ultramarine and violet of the evening sky. But my effort to understand, to see colours the way he saw them, was not enough. The only thing that connected his green with mine was the general concept of green, something like the colour of the grass or trees in Central Park, perhaps not even that. I remember the photographs in the guidebook. The morning after he had told me about his first dream, feeling out of my depth, I went to a bookstore on Forty-Sixth Street and bought a guide to Brazil. There were several different books and I chose the one which had the most colour photographs. I thought it would give me at least a bit of self-confidence in communicating with José. When I opened it, I was immediately struck by an aerial photograph of the jungle: shockingly solid green, like thick

coats of oil paint, it spilled over into black and blue. José
told me he loved the jungle and that he had once spent
six months in Mato Grosso. I laughed and said I had
never seen the jungle, except in the movies, and that it
seemed menacing enough on the screen, like some sort
of huge man-eating organism. He consoled me by saying
he had never seen snow except in the movies. The dirty
slush of New York had been his first experience of it and
there was no way I could conjure up for him the crisp
snow on a mountain slope, a window caked with hoar-
frost or a frozen forest. But it did not console me. When
he mentioned a river, I would imagine a green or lead
grey surface of water. To which he would respond that
rivers are yellow or green like emeralds, and for a moment
it was a game. If only we had had the time, perhaps we
could have overcome this rootedness in separate languages. I think it can be done. But then he would have
been somebody else, and ours would have been some
other relationship. Perhaps the inadequacy of words and
our fear of losing our way in the labyrinth of language, our
fear of misunderstanding, actually fed our mutual hunger
for the body. Sometimes I would be horrified by the
thought that I was living with a man who did not exist,
whom I had invented and who, the way I saw him, was
real only in this apartment, only in New York, only for
me, like an arbitrary version of reality which can easily be
dematerialized.

I can see him now, sitting by the window. The first few
days he often sat by the living-room window overlooking
the street and the houses across the way, as if he knew
that he was entering a prison he would never leave. That
gaze silently clinging to the street, to the buildings opposite, to the bookstore, to the Japanese restaurant, it

disturbed me. I thought it was escapism. In the shimmering rays of sunlight which fell on him like fine rain, his face was both familiar and alien. It was the guidebook face of a complete foreigner: high cheekbones, protruding lips and dark, slightly slanted eyes. His father's family had moved to Brazil from Portugal several hundred years ago. His mother was from a family of German Jews who had fled on the eve of the Second World War. Still, sometimes, when the light fell at a certain angle, his face seemed to contain the suggestion of a dark family secret, perhaps traces of Indian slave girls and their illegitimate children. White women did not arrive in Brazil until two hundred years after the discovery of America. Sometimes, when I looked at him for a long time, I would see another colour burning under his skin. His light complexion would seem a mere illusion then; his full lips, the black glint in his eyes, the small nose and wide nostrils, the slanting forehead, would give him away. From beneath the pale skin would emerge the well-defined shadow of an Indian woman, his otherness which so fascinated me. Not only was he a separate other being, which was painful enough, but he was doubly other – because of language, and because of the world he came from, a world about which I knew nothing.

Later I realized that he had been looking not at the street in New York where he lived, but at the one he had come from, which periodically flashed through his mind like an apparition or a receding shore, losing its sharpness until it turned into a blurred outline of his former life. Such intense concentration on the present made us both doubt whether we had ever really existed somewhere out there, where the voices and signs were growing fainter and fainter.

It happened soon after he had moved in, at a Faculty Club dinner we could not avoid. I saw on the opposite side of the room a tall woman with golden, chestnut-coloured hair. Although José had not yet noticed her, from the way she smiled when she spotted him and the way she crossed the room, choosing the shortest route to her destination, I sensed that she was dangerous. At the time, there was no particular reason for me to think of danger. It had nothing to do with her appearance, though there was something provocative about her brisk, purposeful movements. It had to do with a kind of focused attention, like a hawk which has just caught sight of its prey. My instinct told me that the danger was waiting for me where I did not expect it. 'This is Carmen, my colleague from the Portuguese Department,' José said when she finally reached us. Her eyes flicked past me as if I were an object, the chair on which José was sitting or the glass he was holding, and she began to speak to him in Portuguese.

That instant I recognized the enemy, and I could name it: it was language.

Their language made me invisible. It was territory inaccessible to me, where Carmen and José established contact at once. I saw how José's face changed, how his usual strained attention relaxed. He plunged into the landscape of his own language as he would into something familiar and warm, into comfortable slippers or a hot, scented bath. I was excluded. Although the room was quite small, I felt instantly as if he were miles away, as if he had moved into a far corner of the room. I remember that all I saw among the crowds for most of the evening was the back of his light blue shirt – my eyes followed this blur, which became the focus of all my attention. He stood there, next to her, a glass in his hand, his entire body leaning forward, toward her. I felt his energy brimming over. It made me tremble. She smiled, shaking her long hair. I heard her ringing laugh as José said something. Then he joined in. His laughter slid down my skin and bounced back at him like an echo. My eyes were glued to him. I did not even try to listen – I would not have understood it anyway. What are they talking about? Why is she smiling? I wondered feverishly. Someone touched my arm. I turned slightly, so that I did not lose sight of José. It was G.S., the old professor. I let him put his arm around my waist and whisper something into my ear, but I did not hear what it was. I could not allow myself to take my attention away from José and Carmen even for a second. The old man kept his arm around my waist, I could feel it, but I did nothing to get rid of him; I was paralyzed by a fear that was already rising to my throat. They are talking for too long, I thought, although I did not know how long was too long, or what that might mean exactly. Five minutes? Half an hour? The very presence of someone who could communicate with José in his own language was reason enough to make me panic. But what was I so afraid of, when it was me, not she, who knew the pattern of the moles on his body, the taste of his skin and lips, both morning and night? Nonetheless, in those few moments my fear grew into hate, into the strong silk thread of hate. I saw myself tightening that thread around her throat, which was spilling out words for the last time, the bewitching unknown Portuguese words which were forming an impenetrable circle around José.

What was José seeing and feeling at that moment? What was in the sound of his language? The overcrowded streets of São Paulo, the heat pressing on the skin like lead? The smell of rot, the whiteness of the sand, an excerpt from a novel, the news, the street vendors hawking newspapers? Her voice dissolved inside him into a million images, memories, sounds which surfaced suddenly, like a flood threatening to sweep him out of the room, the city, far away from me. I held the imaginary silk thread in my hand, knowing that I could quite calmly strangle Carmen, cut off her beguiling voice and turn the seduction by language, of which she was not even aware, into a gasping wheeze. But just then José turned away from Carmen. The conversation was over and now his eyes scanned the tables, the walls, the closed windows. I knew he was feeling lost, feeling that he did not belong here. Then his eyes found my face and that calmed him down. He walked over and kissed me lightly on the cheek, as if wondering whether I really existed and which of us, Carmen or me, was the real, live woman. It's stuffy in here, he said, and opened the window.

Later, as we sat together at one of the tables – Carmen was seated to his left but he barely said more than a few words to her – I lifted the tablecloth and looked under the table a few times, without José noticing. I was afraid they might be secretly touching under the table, although I knew that that was not the problem. All I saw was José nervously tapping his foot. I noticed a small hole in his light blue shirt, just under the right shoulder. I thought that I had ironed that shirt several times now, and that this tied us together.

For José and I could barely rely on any language other than that of the body, precisely because we lacked a common language, or found the one we had inadequate. We had no other way to reach each other. Our bodies – touch, gestures, facial expressions, food, sex – became the basis of our communication, our new country, for which, day by day, we composed a precise itinerary. Our only safety lay in the physical mechanism of translating one being into the other. It was the only way that I could understand the language of his emotions. Where words proved powerless, the lexicon of subtle physical signs increased. Now when I watch other people, it strikes me that their exclusive focus on language blinds and deprives them of other possibilities of communication. Losing the ability to read the inner lining of the spoken word reduces people, disables them.

Our words were enveloped in our skin.

'You know how long we've been together? Five days already,' José would say. And then ten, and then thirty. It wasn't that he was counting the days, it was just that the fact amazed him. Time was obviously no longer a straight line, but an elusive curve, a room with countless mirrors. The days did not add up, they multiplied, peeled away, dispersed in all directions, and every time we turned around or stopped we became all the more certain of it. We knew that we had a finite amount of time to spend together, but once we plunged into it (I thought of it as a lake), that became quite irrelevant. We lived in a kind of distorted, insane time of our own. And so now, when I try to reconstruct the time we spent together, I can't. Sometimes I think of it all as one day, as an integral whole, as a sticky ball of dough. I would like to remember everything we did, but the sequence of events simply eludes me, as if someone had deprived me of the ability to put my recollections into chronological order, and had simply left me with a mass of random images and scenes. I think I must be suffering from a special kind of oblivion: my memory is contracting into a brilliant beam of light which, like a spotlight in the theatre, illuminates only particular scenes. The only thing I can trust is my corporeal memory, the memory inscribed on the inner side of my thigh, under my arm, behind my ear, in the palm of my hand.

It surfaces suddenly, when I least expect it.

IV

The day before yesterday, having spent the entire afternoon wiping the apartment clean of even the slightest, microscopic trace of dirt – exaggerated fastidiousness which, I must admit, took up a lot of time – I decided to treat myself to a luxurious bath with Kniepp's rosemary oil to relax my aching muscles. And that instant I found myself slipping into the same scented bath in Dubrovnik. My father was appearing at the Dubrovnik Summer Festival. We were spending the summer in Madame Maria's villa beyond the city's western gate. The villa was surrounded by a high wall. Two tall palm trees stood on either side of the front door, and in the back garden a pine tree cast its shade into my room, making it darker and cooler than the rest of the house. The stone-flagged path down to the sea was bordered with bushes of pink and yellow oleander, and I remember the fragrance of myrtle, and a rosemary bush branching out under the bathroom window. Before my evening bath, my mother would reach out of the window, snap off a sprig of rosemary and soak it in the tepid water. To make my little girl sleep better, she would say and go off, humming, to dress for the concert, leaving me in the bath of scented water. Then Tonci, Madame Maria's son, would come in. He would enter quietly, carefully leaving the door slightly ajar, just enough to allow him to hear my mother's footsteps or her voice when she called me to dinner. Madame Maria took pride in telling us that Tonci was studying to be a sea captain, like his late father. Just like his father, she would say, glancing at the framed photograph of a man in a captain's uniform hanging on the living-room wall. I do not remember Tonci's face, I just know that he was blonde. I was six or seven years old. He would kneel next to the tub and dip his hand in the water. 'Be a good girl,' he would whisper. 'You're a good girl who's going to bed now, and I've just come to wish you goodnight. You're not afraid of me. You're not afraid, are you? You know that your Uncle Tonci has come to say goodnight. I just want to tickle you a little, but you won't tell anybody, because if you do, in the morning I'll throw you into the deep well out in the garden. But no, no, you won't tell anybody – you like it,' he would murmur, slipping his index finger up between my legs. First he would stroke me slowly, and then faster and faster. Sometimes it lasted for a while, sometimes not – it depended on my mother. I thought of the well with its rusty lid. I watched his big hand moving under the water like some sea animal, and I inhaled the smell of the rosemary until I was overcome with heat, and then with pleasant cramps. When he heard my mother's footsteps on the stairs, he would leap out of the window in a single bound and disappear. Later he would dine with us and say little. Now, when I think about it, he was probably shy.

At the end of the garden was the beach, but because of the steep drop of the rocks into the sea I was not allowed to go swimming alone. Tonci offered to take me, and my parents gladly agreed, because that meant that at the hottest time of day they could retire to their bedroom and take a nap in peace and quiet. Tonci let me dive and stay in the water until my lips turned blue, and only when I was frozen stiff did he make me come out and dry off on the slab of stone. I would lie there in the sun, a faint pink light penetrating my eyelids, a cricket trilling somewhere in the grass, and Tonci would lick the salt off my shoulders, stomach and legs. I'm going to eat you all up, eat you all up, he would say, and I would giggle because his tongue tickled me. I'm going to start with these little toes, then for my main course I'll have this leg, and last of all there's dessert, he would say, sliding his tongue into the cleft between my legs. I remember the soft pressure of his tongue and the taste of sweat on my upper lip, I remember the rush of the sea which was soon drowned out by the rush of my breathing.

The first time José's tongue touched me in that same spot as I was lying in bed in the darkness of his room, I suddenly thought I could hear the sea again after all those years. Quite distinctly, somewhere nearby, the waves were washing the rock on which I was lying. The same thing has been happening to me again now, when my memory of him suddenly comes alive in some part of my body. It must be José reminding me that I am still completely in his power. My memory, my feelings, my flesh, me, that is all his now, all his. He decides everything, he controls everything. Never again will I be my own master.

After my rosemary-oil bath I reached for the baby oil. José had taught me to rub oil on my skin while it was still wet from my bath, because the skin absorbs it better that way and stays silky for a long time. But as my wet hand glided down my own skin, it was as if my fingers were running down his skin, not my finely shaped muscles. His soft, warm, slippery skin. He was lying on his stomach, half asleep, putting himself completely in my hands, which moved in circles across the thin layer of oil, one minute touching him gently as if dissolving him, and the next squeezing hard his shoulders, neck, arms, the calves of his legs, as if I wanted to rip them off, to separate them from the bones. The shape of his body imprinted on my fingers flashed so brightly for a second that I had to ask myself whether I would be able to live like this, whether I could stand the way in which José was being resurrected in me, and the way I missed him. My desire for his kiss was so strong that in my pulse I could feel the blood rising to my lips, until they were swollen. As I lay in bed waiting for sleep to come, I thought I could hear his careful tread, the quiet steps of his bare feet on the wooden floor. He stood at the head of my bed, only the rhythm of his breathing and his smell betraying him. It was the barely audible breathing of someone holding his breath. I caught a whiff of the fresh smell of soap, the smell of tobacco on his fingers, the smell of his armpits. He took another step and laid his lips upon mine. He touched me only with his lips and his tongue. Once again, all of him entered me through the thin mucous membrane. I slid my hand between my legs, as Tonci once used to do.

Yes, what I remember and cannot forget, because it is not up to me, what keeps coming back, is the feeling of desire: that inner hotness of the being, that total focus, the blood throbbing at José's every real or imaginary touch.

It bothered me that I could not concentrate properly on the cleaning. When I finally got around to doing the kitchen, I kept going back into the bedroom, even though

I had cleaned that already. With my open suitcase packed, the room looked empty, like a hotel room just before you check out. The books had been mailed off earlier. I had wanted to take advantage of having José take them to the post office, because the box was so heavy that I could not budge it on my own. The only thing I held on to was the guidebook to Brazil. It was the one book I did not want to be parted from. In the box I also packed away my doctoral thesis, unfinished of course, with all my notes, photocopies and the books I had managed to find. Because in the end I think I will finish it, though it will take me a while to find my feet in Warsaw again. It may not be until next spring. First I want to take care of Father. His health is deteriorating, his voice on the phone sounds reedy somehow, thin. Arthritis has started giving him serious trouble and I wonder how much longer he will be able to give even piano lessons, and not lapse into complete resignation and solitude. He has not been the same since Mother died anyway. He has become withdrawn, he barely communicates with anyone and he eats poorly. Jadwiga comes twice a week to clean the apartment and cook a few days' worth of lunch for him, but she often returns to find the food untouched. At least that is what she said when I called home once and she answered the phone. I could easily imagine Father sitting in the armchair by the phone, wearing his crimson-and-black-striped dressing gown, barely able to hold the receiver in his sick hands, his voice raised in excitement as he told me about his hands, the weather, the neighbours.

With the approach of my departure date, images from my previous life are slowly starting to return to me. But it was not until it was all over that the thought of the future emerged from the mist, a thought which, until four days ago, had been banished from my life. To think about the future implied life without José, and as soon as we met that had seemed absolutely pointless. We could not continue to live apart. We had both been aware of this sentence almost from the beginning, although we had not fully understood what it meant. In entering this apartment, we were both entering another life. Our previous lives suddenly turned into the distant past which occasionally upset us, bothered us and dragged us down toward some kind of invisible abyss. Now and then the leaden weights of the past would slow our movement through the streets of New York. I recognized that same heaviness in the confused steps of the Poles, Czechs or Russians walking in the Village, turning round, stopping at every shop window, so slow and awkward that they constantly seemed to be banging into people in the street. The past needed to be forgotten, it needed to be switched off. Like when you turn off the electricity fuse box in your apartment and suddenly everything goes pitch dark.

It was not hard for me to switch off my previous life, even before I met José. The mail was slow and the phone lines were bad. There was always a humming sound in the receiver, as if the sea was coming in. You would often get cut off, and anyway it was expensive to phone home. My new reality absorbed me completely. The sense of being separated from my life in Warsaw was so great that I could even imagine not going back there. I could imagine that for some inner reason it became harder and harder for me to go back. I did not talk to Barbara so often any more, and she was a friend I had not only grown up with but previously could barely survive the day without. Suddenly, the longer I was in New York, the more my conversations with her became a tiresome obligation. She would give me detailed reports on the subject of Marek and his new girl-friend, or politics, or her affair with her boss, which she seemed simply unable to end (she worked in the unversity library). As she talked, I knew that she was sitting on the couch in her mother's apartment, her hair in curlers, wear-ing a blue tracksuit. Barbara dyed her hair regularly, her desire to be a blonde transcending all criticism. It's vulgar, my mother would tell her, like not shaving under your arms. But Barbara would not be dissuaded; what is more, I had to help her bleach it. The fact that her hair would stink of ammonia later, especially when wet, was of no con-cern to her. 'Men like blondes,' was her only comment, and she was right. To break off my relationship with her was like cutting my umbilical cord with Poland. But I simply started avoiding conversations with her. I could not find the right way to share my new reality with her. Maybe because it was becoming harder and harder to find com-parisons with her life in Warsaw. I mean, I soon realized that people here do not bleach their hair with peroxide or ammonia, and so it does not smell so bad. As time passed, the incomparability of our experiences increasingly iso-lated me from Barbara, as if my mouth was closing of its own accord. My silences in our phone conversations became longer and longer, and Barbara finally stopped sneaking calls from her office at the library, and even stopped writing to me. I knew that she was offended, that she thought I was not coming back. My colleagues at the institute thought so too, and I even received a letter from the director, cautiously inquiring about my plans and my return home. My plans? Home? Curlers, housecoats, the smell of damp and dust, wilting vegetables. What could I tell him? How could I describe the way I was anchored in this new reality?

José and I were sitting in a café at the bottom of Fifth Avenue the day after I received the anxious letter from the institute. I completely understood the director's concern. So many Poles had emigrated. In the early days I sometimes went to see Elzbieta and Leszek, who had also come to New York on grants and had stayed on. But they continued to read Polish newspapers, listen to the *Voice of America* in Polish and cook Polish dishes – Elzbieta made the best *krupnik* in the world. They lived two streets away, between First and Second Avenue, where there are lots of Polish and Ukrainian shops. At the party they threw to celebrate getting their American citizenship all the guests were Poles, except for about three and a half Americans. As soon as José moved in with me I stopped visiting them.

When that rough brown paper envelope with its faculty logo and Polish stamp arrived, I did not tell José. It had become difficult to talk about our other lives. If he did refer to his wife, he would immediately pass over every letter of her name with a long silence, like a sponge. Occasionally he would mention his son, but even Felipe seemed to be fading away, as if he had already become a memory. He confused my cat's name with my father's, and I laughed. It didn't matter. All that mattered was the colour of the sky above, and the way his eyes reflected it.

The sole purpose of my existence was to see that hue and taste the grated chocolate on top of the whipped cream in my wide, shallow cup of coffee.

All I could say in reply to the director's letter was how much it meant to read my own language, how much of my country I could feel in the familiar words and phrases. But even that would have been difficult for me to explain. I felt as if I were on a ship which was rapidly sailing away from shore. It was not that I had forgotten my native tongue, but that I had been forced to give up its most important part, the part which expresses emotions. I was living on the dry, narrow terrain of English, where I could not move freely. It was as if my language and I were not inhabiting the same dimension of reality. Somewhere in the middle of me, an emptiness was growing. And with it so was my chance of returning. But I had not realized that yet.

The one link with home that I had not renounced was prayer. Every evening I would say to myself the words I had learned by heart and which had been a part of me since childhood. They were impossible to forget. They would always come to mind and transport me back to my room, to our church on a chilly Sunday morning, to my mother's side. Once we even made the pilgrimage to the Black Virgin at Czestochowa. I was maybe five when my mother took me on the pilgrimage. We went by bus, and then on foot to the church. It was a sultry, humid day. We walked in a long column, our steps slow and steady. My mother was talking to a woman who was leading her sixteen-year-old handicapped son by the hand. The entire way the boy's mouth hung open and his eyes rolled up to the sky. 'He's better,' the woman said. 'I can see that he's better already.' My mother had brought along a basket of walnut cakes and elderberry juice. The smell of the walnuts and the burning candles, the soft murmur of the pilgrims, the singing which grew louder as we approached the clearing where mass was to be held, the voice of the priest coming through the megaphone, telling groups from the different towns where to assemble, the candied-apples vendor running alongside the procession shouting, 'Apples! Apples! Sweet apples!' It all rose from the depths of me, stirring inside me, refusing to let me go, to let me finally belong only to José. Sometimes I would say the prayer aloud, experiencing an almost physical pleasure in the sweet repetition of the familiar words. They tasted like meringue, melting slowly in the mouth. Perhaps those evening prayers were my only defence against the destructive oblivion into which I was sinking, where everything that penetrated from the outside, from the past, was immediately perceived as hostile.

V

With each day José and I progressively inhabited each other. How else could we recognize our desires if not by listening to them from within? How else could we have known what we thought or how we saw the world if not by finding a way to be together, to belong to each another completely? I felt that if I gave up my own past, if I reduced my self-awareness to brief fleeting moments, I just might be able to do it. Sometimes, though, I was terrified by the way I felt that my body no longer belonged to me alone, by the way in which I was defined in relation to José. I recognized it in the little things and, from time to time, when I became aware of it, I would feel an irrevocable loss. I could barely be sure any more that I was doing anything for myself. Even when buying jeans, I caught myself looking at my image from the outside as I tried them on, as if I was stepping completely outside myself to check whether the jeans fit properly. Fit not me, but the body I recognized as me one minute, and the next saw merely as a receptacle into which we were both being poured. At the same time, I felt that by stepping out of myself I was doing what I had to do – taking another stride toward becoming a new being.

Sometimes I observed myself with my own eyes, and sometimes with his. A week ago, when José was still alive, I decided to buy a dress I had seen earlier in a shop window on Madison Avenue. It was a simple black jersey sheath. I had everything planned already and wanted something formal for 'the day after', something like a widow's dress, but one that would emphasize my figure. I went shopping alone, José stayed behind in one of his increasingly frequent stupors, teetering between drunkenness and unconsciousness, and I did not even try to rouse him because at this stage his condition made my task easier. The little shop was empty and I felt a kind of joyful intimacy in the fact that the saleswoman could devote herself entirely to me. When I tried on the dress and stood in front of the mirror, the saleswoman gave me a long, appraising look. 'It's perfect on you,' she said. Her words sounded so convincing, as if she really was talking about me, as if I could completely trust the independent existence her look had given me – like a medal or brooch to go with the dress, I thought.

Just when I was sure that I had, for a moment at least, shed this sensation of absence from my own body, José's eyes awaited me where I least expected them: in my hair ribbon. Along with the dress I had meant to buy a black velvet ribbon, to add to my appearance of mourning. Death, the physical death of another human being, necessitates, formally anyway, a period of mourning. And so I had decided that for a while at least I would wear black and the ribbon. But when I put the ribbon in my hair, my face changed beyond recognition. I thought it must be the circles under my eyes from lack of sleep – José would wake up at night and throw himself feverishly on top of me – but it was not that. I noticed a strange, slight relaxation, an attenuation of my face in the mirror. Framed by the black ribbon, you could see that the face lacked a centre. That moment I felt, as clearly as a needle piercing my brain, that I was looking at myself through his eyes. José was observing me through my pupils, staring at that softness, that spill of live tissue. He looked carefully at my naked face, a face which was eluding him, which he no longer recognized. For an instant he thought he was seeing his own reflection in the mirror, but then he saw that paleness framed in black, like a light stain on the water's surface. I yanked off the ribbon, as if wanting, with that one movement, to peel the skin off my face.

Although he was still alive, I already felt him inside me. I was already doubled by his heavy presence. It was a bewildering feeling at first. However much I wanted us to merge into a single being, his direct presence inside me, his devouring of me from within, startled and frightened me. That must be how a pregnant woman feels, except that pregnancy is finite. From now on I will be condemned always to feel every slightest movement of another being inside me, that heavy burden of his flesh in my stomach.

But that was what I wanted; that was what I had been dreaming about these past weeks, that feeling of weight and fullness when the man inside me turns into my own unborn child.

Yesterday I washed the tub, the sink and the bathroom tiles. I poured a liquid into the toilet to dissolve the limescale, but I still had to clean the bowl with a brush. I felt good as I reached under the rim of the bowl and scrubbed until all trace of the yellow scale had gone. I had never thought I would be able to kneel down, and stick my hand inside a toilet bowl and find a certain enjoyment in

doing so. Still, it was not hard for me to get down on my
knees and scrub the floor around the bathtub, or to wipe
the tiles with Ajax until they sparkled. I remembered that
Jadwiga used to dip a rag in vinegar when she washed our
old white tiles with their blue floral border, and afterwards
the bathroom would smell like cucumber salad.

The cleaner the apartment, the more exhausted I became.
But physical fatigue made me feel good. With my hand
stuck deep in the toilet I did not have to think about the
past or the future.

At around one o'clock I left for a lunch date at the
Russian Tea Room. Rebecca, whom I had met in Warsaw
the year before, had invited me the week before. It was a
cold, sunny day, and it smelled of snow, which had started
to fall the previous night. I came out of the subway and
walked west along Fifty-Seventh Street with a light heart,
almost proudly, like someone who has accomplished a
job. The red leather chairs, uniformed waiters, gold and
purple colours everywhere, and the fact that I was with
other people, that I finally noticed them, filled me with
unexpected delight. Rebecca had recently returned from
Warsaw. She had seen Barbara, of course, and had visited
my father and taken him a jar of Nescafé as a present.
'He's holding up well,' she said, 'though he's maybe a bit
depressed.' She went on to discuss other common
acquaintances with the kind of enthusiasm only a tourist
can have. I tried to follow her; I would have gladly listened to her attentively, especially as I had a confirmed
seat on the plane back to Warsaw only forty-eight hours
later. I almost told her, it almost slipped out: why, I'm
travelling the day after tomorrow. But caution stopped
me. Complications could still arise. I might not manage
to finish everything in time. Anyway, I was still here, and

in my mind I had not made the break between here and there. 'And you, you look different somehow,' said Rebecca. 'You've changed. You're so beautiful. You're glowing, glowing from inside. Are you in love?' Her question threw me. Picking up my silver knife to spread a pat of cold butter on a slice of rye bread, I listened to her with one ear. 'Am I in love? Yes, of course I am,' I confessed immediately. I think I even lowered my eyes. I should not have done that, because just then the dark red borscht arrived on the table. The colour made me uncomfortable: it was too soon after what had happened, somehow. It reminded me of the watery blood at the bottom of the bathtub. But the tart tang of the beetroot soup on my palate dispelled my unease. Everything is fine, I thought; everything is perfect, in fact. I am forgetting José, and that is good. He does not exist outside me and his blood is not gushing into the bathtub any more. At the moment it is dissolving inside me just like the beetroot soup. Now that I was no longer obsessed with the unbearable fear of being separated from José, everything seemed so simple. 'You will forget me,' he used to say, looking into my eyes as if it were easier for him to confront that oblivion then, at the very beginning. But what José did not realize, and what I felt like a chill wind in the face, was that he was talking about oblivion as if it were death. He was equating the two. I will die when you forget me.

He did say 'will', not 'if'.

The end and death had been built into this relationship from the beginning, like invisible threads which connected us – that feeling of danger, of transgression, of union which is in itself transgression. As if this immeasurable corporality, this immersion and permeation of our bodies, was merely the connecting tissue of death. We were connected by death. But how could I tell Rebecca any of this?

The end is my hands under the tap of hot running water, it is the dirty dishes still waiting in the sink to be washed. A cloudy sky. The smell of stale food. I knew that it was the end by the sense of peace which filled me as I cleaned the kitchen yesterday, by the sort of pleasant exhaustion that overcame me as I sipped my afternoon tea. In some other situation I would have said it was plain fatigue, but actually I was full of energy, even slightly fired up by the rush. I still had to make it to midnight mass. But at least I did not feel that tension any more, or those cramps in my stomach before making the final decision. I did not feel torn between the awareness that the transgression was necessary and the desire for total possession of and union with José. I was horrified by the ravenous hunger of this frenzy of love inside me which I was unable to fight, and which only the object of its adoration could satiate. Yet at the same time I felt the self-confidence of a priest performing a precise, prescribed rite.

I am convinced that José knew I would find a way out and that he put himself into my hands, into the eternity I embodied. I think he guessed I was planning something, though I was very careful and cleverly hid from him all the tools I needed. For instance, I kept the big wooden chopping board in the basement. José did not go down there any more. I stashed the other instruments in the pantry, under the potatoes and onions. We had so much food you would have thought we were planning to stay in this apartment forever. The shelves were stacked with cans of peas and peeled tomatoes, flour and different kinds of pasta. A whole, barely touched twine of garlic and a string of hot red chilli peppers hung from the door. Only later did I realize that this pantry reminded me of the one we had at home. I wonder why I had not noticed that before. Perhaps I had, perhaps one of the reasons why I had stocked up so much food was precisely that fear that we would be left without sugar or oil, a fear I could not shake off, even in New York.

My mother had a rule – in our house she always had a rule for everything – that the pantry had to be full at all times. The stocks always had to be replenished. As if war were going to break out tomorrow, my father would say, albeit not too loudly. She was right, of course: it was the only way to survive in a country where your lunch was decided by chance, never by imagination. There always had to be sausages, and at least some ham. Jadwiga's husband Pavel took care of that. He usually raised two pigs for our needs. Father thought that was too much. 'Then go and find sausages and ham in Warsaw yourself, if that's what you think,' Mother would tell him, revealing a sometimes surprising practicality. He would not embark on such a complicated and uncertain venture, but he did bring food home from his various trips abroad. He also brought perfume, soaps, cosmetics and underwear. My mother had a passion for silk, lacy underwear, something I discovered when she was already very ill and had no plain underwear for the hospital – she thought it unseemly to wear silk there. Apart from underwear, she also asked him to bring her back Swiss chocolate with hazelnuts, the plain Milka which we ate ourselves, and the finer variety for guests. He brought back bitter English marmalade, Marmite, Twinings teas, smoked salmon and herrings, Hungarian sausages, cheeses from France and Denmark, cognac, champagne and sometimes even bananas. In a way it saddened me that all the things my father had brought back and offered so proudly to his guests could be found here at any corner supermarket. But we actually lived off those fifty kilos of peas, sackloads of potatoes, heads of plain and pickled cabbage (which we kept on the balcony because of the smell) and canisters of who knows how much flour and oil. There was also a crate or two of apples, each wrapped in newspaper. On the shelves was powdered milk and at least a kilo of coffee – still green, unroasted and unground so it would last longer. Neatly arranged on the shelves were the glass jars of pickles, pickled peppers and jam. Barbara's mother pickled the vegetables and made excellent plum jam. My mother always kept at least a few kilos of corn groats for me. I had tried polenta as a child, and after that ate it often. That had been at the summer festival in Spoleto, where we had stayed with a friend of my father's, a violinist who had a hillside cottage above the city. I discovered polenta in New York only recently, in a healthfood store, where I paid two and a half dollars for half a kilo.

I was surprised to hear that José like polenta too; they had often had it at his grandfather's *fazenda* in Bahia. It was cooked by black retainers who were no longer slaves but had stayed on as servants. José and I would sometimes make it for dinner, pouring milk or yoghurt over it and eating it from the same plate. If there was any left in the morning, we would dice it up and fry it in butter for breakfast. We would both happily bite into the yellow cubes, glad that we at least had the taste of polenta in common. Whereas all too easily we left the present outside the apartment door – it was enough to simply close the door, not answer the phone or letters, not talk about outside things – the past would crop up almost daily through food.

Apart from my mother's wartime rules for filling the pantry, José and I had requirements of our own. Once a week, on Saturdays usually, we would go to Dean & Deluca on Broadway to stock up. We took pleasure in every article – in the wine vinegar, the young goat's cheese, the basil (I planted it in a jar on the windowsill, which is where I will leave it), the black beans. We had to go elsewhere to get the dried tongue for *feijoada*, the palm oil and *mandioca*, but José had brought with him to New York the address of a store which sold it. José was an excellent cook. We bought an earthenware dish in which he prepared meat or beans or fish, and always hot, *quente*. Living with him I had become used to the taste, which burns the mouth and is then washed down with a tall glass of beer.

We cooked together every day. It was a ritual, like making love, and no less important. Cooking took the place of conversation. It was a way for us to learn about each other. José liked hot, salty, very spicy food. He found the way I cooked meat or vegetables 'pale'. He meant, of course, bland. Hovering over the pot, he would list the ingredients of a good *feijoada,* explain how he made it, the way he had been taught by his grandfather's cook, who was said to be the last of the old man's mistresses. She had moved in with them when José was about fifteen. He was the only one in the family who had learned how to cook. Not even his mother, a slim, blonde Jew (you remind me of her, he sometimes told me), had learned how to cook Creole food.

Antonia, the cook, was an enormous black woman with a white lace kerchief on her head and strings of colourful necklaces to protect her against evil spirits. If someone was in the kitchen, it was her custom to describe what she was doing aloud. Obviously this was something José had picked up from her. Since he pottered around the kitchen more than anyone else, she treated him like an apprentice. She took his culinary education very seriously. 'You do not leave talent to chance,' she would say. When he managed to make something by himself, she would clutch him to her breasts, as round and heavy as big watermelons – a moment José could hardly wait for. Her breasts smelled of food, he told me, of cinnamon, nutmeg and lemon. In her cleavage the heavy smell of garlic mingled with the fragrance of coconut and bamboo liqueur, which every so often Antonia would sip straight from the bottle. Sometimes, when he was sure no one was at home, he would teasingly slip his hand inside her blouse, then pull out her breast and press his lips against the nipple, like a child wanting to be nursed. Antonia, who must have been around forty at the time, did not stop him. 'Eat,' she would say, 'eat, eat. I've fed so many children already.' Her nipples were like chocolate cookies or big, dark figs. His mouth was full. 'I felt as if I could drown in my own voraciousness,' José said.

For a while, after he had left his parents' home, he had dreamed that he was choking on Antonia's nipples. It was such a sweet death, he told me pensively, as if wishing for it. Sometimes he would bare my breasts. Not because they reminded him of Antonia's – mine are quite small with barely visible pale nipples. He did it because it excited him to make love quickly and suddenly in the kitchen, near the food, next to the stove or on the table. For him there was a strong, direct connection between sex and food, as if the one reminded him of the other. I noticed it our very first night together in his room. Later, I would be the one to initiate the game. When we cooked, I would feed him pieces of boiled vegetables from the soup, or freshly toasted bread, or take the food from his plate and feed him with my fingers. As he took the food from my hands, his eyes closed, it was like completely erasing the border between food and body, my body. My fingers dissolved in his mouth and themselves became food, sliding down the throat which hungrily swallowed them. The words I uttered then were no longer enough. I spoke to him through my fingers; through the tip of my tongue, which entered his ear with the sound of my words; through my saliva; through the warmth of my lips, the sharpness of my teeth, which nibbled him like a cracker; through my rambling murmurings of excitement. And then he would respond, with his whole body he would say the same thing: I love you, I love you, I love you. I felt his breath slip through his vocal chords and enter me like a serpent made of panting air, mucous and the desperate need to penetrate me through my every opening. For me to absorb his dissolving voice. For him to be inside me, at last.

To end in me.

In the beginning, our time was night, darkness, benumbed consciousness curled up at the edge of the precipice, when we would drown in each other and the gap between us would completely disappear. Our bodies functioned like two perfect pleasure-producing machines.

Pleasure, then sleep. Like death.

Never before had death been so close to pleasure for me. The thought of death which came to me before I fell asleep from physical exhaustion was so light and billowy, like a thin black veil fluttering with our breath. To die like that, united in a small black nucleus of eternity. When I tried to say something, he would put his hand over my mouth. He was afraid of my whisper, of the words I did not speak but which were there, between our moist, dissolving bodies. Later, when we began to cook together, our time was no longer restricted merely to the night. During the day, in the kitchen, words would turn into juicy bites of roast leg of lamb, potatoes, crab soup, fish in dill sauce and chocolate cake. It was as if through food we were slowly shedding the fear of misunderstanding. But we simply could not, could not get enough of each other. When I mentioned this to him, when I told him that nothing could satiate my hunger for him, he quoted Marie Bonaparte to me. Even though they were in Portuguese, I understood the words:

O amor é o mais exigente, o mais difícil de satisfazer dos nossos instintos. Temos fome e se podemos comer, a fome desaparece. Temos sede e se podemos beber, cessamos de ter sede. Temos sono e se dormimos nós despertamos bem dispostos. Assim repousados, saciados, despertos, não pensamos mais em comer, beber ou dormir, até que a necessidade de novo renasça. Mas a necessidade de amor e de uma tenacidade diferente, parace-se com uma sede que ninquém poderá satisfazer totalmente, nem mesmo pela posse física.

How I love the sound of these words now as I say them aloud.

José's story about Antonia did not upset me. As far as I was concerned, it was as if none of the women who had imprinted their being on his skin before me had ever existed. They belonged to another, distant time and life and were connected to us only in some nebulous, undefined way, like pictures which surface in our dreams but whose meaning we cannot quite decipher, and so we soon forget them. José knew that, too, which was why it did not worry him to talk about them. That is how he came to tell

71

me about Consuelo, I don't remember now in what context. Consuelo was his wife's sister, one of five, the youngest. He and Inês had only just married when they went with her entire family to spend the summer in a house on the beach. Inês, pregnant and suffering from morning sickness, returned to São Paulo with the rest of her family. José stayed behind in the house – classes had not yet started at the university. Consuelo stayed behind as well. Their first night alone in the house he heard footsteps and then the door of his room slowly opened. Consuelo stood there naked in the moonlight reflected off the sea. 'I did not recognize her,' José told me. 'She was a different person.' Standing there in front of him was an adult woman who had made an important decision, not the sixteen-year-old sister of his wife. He got up and took her by the hand. They went out on to the beach. The sand was still hot. They made love in the sea. Her body was fresh and firm. 'She slid through my hands like a fish.' Passion cannot be explained, José told me. They spent three days together in the house on the beach. When he got back home, he told his wife and her parents. They took it relatively calmly: it was Consuelo growing up, and José had turned her into a woman. Inês too forgave him – that is to say, she did not hold it against him too much. José thought he was one of those men to whom such things simply happened. Women appeared out of the blue and threw themselves at him, like the young woman journalist, some of his female students or his boss, who wanted to leave her husband for José. He was convinced that these light affairs left no scars. He did not realize that with every such encounter he risked the possibility of real change, madness, suicide, murder. By the time José understood that every affair was dangerous, because every touch of love was a union of death and life, it was too late.

Maybe your attitude to women is different when the first woman you ever slept with was a prostitute in a whorehouse where you had been taken, as was the custom, by an uncle or male relative. José remembered that it had been a two-storey house with a porch, and that he could hear music playing inside. When they stepped in out of the sun-drenched street they were washed by a wave of semi-darkness in which he could barely tell apart the faces of the women and the men. It was early afternoon and the house seemed to be just waking up. They climbed up the wooden stairs, its carpet held in place by brass rods, and entered a room. His uncle pushed him inside through the gold-threaded brocade crimson curtain. He still remembered those big gold roses on the curtain, as if they were the features of the experience most deeply imprinted on his memory. The only light seeped in through the closed shutters. A woman was lying on the high bed. He thought she was asleep. He stepped back but his uncle, who was standing behind him, pushed him on into the room. He could not remember the woman's face, just the tiny lilies on the wallpaper and the fringe on the canopy. On the little night table was a small plaster statue of the Virgin Mary, adorned with dried flowers, the only familiar object in that stuffy, frighteningly dark, unknown womb of a room. He took several steps toward the bed and then stopped. The woman still seemed to be sleeping, her face buried in the pillow. He saw only her hair – long, dark and still. He could feel the sweat on his loins. Excitement mingled with fear, and he thought that any minute he would throw up on the rug in front of the bed, that he already reeked of sour vomit. And then the woman held out her hand, a dark, full hand with bright red nails. She pulled him toward her. He climbed on to the bed and with a single deft movement she had him inside her. He plunged into something hot and moist and then, then he was carried away. All he remembered was that he cried, and her soothing hand on his face. He fell asleep on top of her. He did not know how long he slept. He was woken by the pungent smell of her body. Her back was turned to him, her big naked body occupying almost the entire bed. José was astonished by how small he felt. He tried to crawl out of the bed but she turned and clasped him in her arms once more. When he went out, his hands smelled of her. His uncle was waiting for him, lounging in the rocking chair on the porch. He was smoking a cigar. It was already dark. 'Good,' he said. 'Now you are a man.'

'I was thirteen,' said José.

As he told me the story I could just imagine him, that sudden sprout of a thirteen-year-old, his arms too long, his neck too long, in the darkened room filled by the body of a faceless woman. Standing there, waiting. Nobody had told him what was expected of him, what he was supposed to do. These things are not said. And so all he could do was wait for the big woman to turn her attention to him. All he could do was stare at the floor, at the statue of the Virgin Mary or at the pattern on the wallpaper. The memory was distilled into that picture of the room and the anonymous woman in it. Without words, it all happened without words.

I remembered myself in Jan's apartment, in the chilly room which looked like a deserted ballroom. In the corner is a big concert piano, open. The surrounding walls are hung with paintings of relatives: a man with a sabre, a cavalry officer with twirling moustaches. Above the piano, in a heavy gilded frame, is the portrait of Madam Danuta, the opera singer, Jan's mother. Her breasts spill over the tight ribbing of her purple dress. The curtains at the window billow in the breeze. A fire is burning in the tiled stove in the corner. I ask Jan to turn the heat up. Jan is a student of my father's. I practise the piano with him. I am seventeen. He has just graduated from the music academy, he is tall and blond, with finely shaped hands, long, bony fingers and a voice that to me makes him sound even older than he is. We are alone in the apartment – Madam Danuta is often out. We sit side by side on the piano bench and practise. Jan slips his arm around my waist. I continue to play as though nothing is happening. With his other hand he unbuttons my white, hand-knitted mohair pullover. I keep on practising an *étude*. I dare not stop now because this is the only way I feel safe. Jan's fingers play with my nipples, and then remove my clothes, piece by piece. I play until he lowers his head into my lap, until my hands drop from excitement. Jan scoops me up into his arms and carries me to the couch. The piano has fallen silent and in the silence I hear the clock strike the hour in the next room. Three o'clock. At five minutes past three Jan is inside me. It does not hurt too much. A small, barely noticeable bloodstain remains on the green slipcover.

After that, instead of the piano room, we would go to his bedroom twice a week, a room filled with books, music sheets, fishing gear and a bicycle, and we would climb into the unbearably squeaky bed. A year later he emigrated to France, and I was relegated to the clumsy, aggressive paws of my fellow students, to their selfish lips, their miserable ignorance which slowly, almost imperceptibly, made me lose touch with my own body.

*

Without José the kitchen was a sad, absolutely meaningless place, and it was even sadder when I thought of him leaning against the sink or the stove. Perhaps it was only at moments like these that I could admit to myself that I missed him, that I physically missed his presence, our cooking together, his laughter as we tried out some new recipe. Which was probably why I had put off cleaning it for as long as I could. I had left it for the end. The window, with its thin, greasy, sticky film of grime, the tiled floor and wooden table, and the tools I had used – the big wooden chopping board, the kitchen knives and the electric saw. Yesterday I cleaned the saw thoroughly and then returned it to the hardware store where I had bought it. I have learned to keep all my receipts, because Americans have the good custom of letting you exchange or even return your purchases within a week. I exchanged the saw for a good Braun mixer, which I will take back with me to Warsaw. I could not think of anything better. As for the big chopping board, first I soaked it in chlorine to bleach out the dark red bloodstains, then I scrubbed it with a steel pad. Unfortunately, the ugly saw cuts remained. Sometimes, out of my own pure clumsiness, I had cut too deep. I had no experience of handling such a tool. In the end I threw the board away in the garbage. It did not seem right to leave it in such a damaged condition for the next tenant.

When it came to the floor, I saw that the small octagonal tiles were old and cracked and that in places entire chunks were missing. That floor had always looked dirty to me, no matter how often I swept and washed it. And not with the stupid contraptions they use here for washing floors, the sponges and string mops attached to a rod with their complicated mechanisms for wringing them dry, just so you do not have to get your hands wet. These gadgets did only a superficial job of cleaning. They did not get at the mud in the corners. I washed the floor in the only proper way, on my hands and knees, with a rag soaked in hot water mixed with strong detergent. Then I rinsed it with clean water and now you can eat off the floor, as they say. I had never been aware how much dirt bothered me until I came here and saw this sterile, scented, superficial cleanliness – the sprays, the liquids, the powders, the sponges. I took as much care as I could not to soil the apartment, but it was not easy to handle a human body without making a pigsty out of the place. I was not that agile, and besides, I knew I would have to clean everything anyway. There would probably have been less of a mess had I had some experience with animals, even if it was just slaughtering a chicken. It did occur to me at one point to call in a cleaning agency and pay for someone to at least do the heavy-duty part of the job, but the apartment was in such a state that I could not let anyone in it.

Now I am glad I saw it through, and, tired as I am, at least I know I did it all myself.

I was used to waking up in strange beds, next to men sleeping on their backs, with their mouths hopelessly open, when I met Piotr. Piotr was a painter who lived in the village of Podkowa Lesna, in a little wooden house which must once have been a barn, because it consisted only of one large room, which was his kitchen, his bedroom and his studio all rolled into one. The toilet was outside in the courtyard, and right behind the house were the woods. I can see Piotr now, sitting in the house, inhaling the smell of turpentine and painting forest monsters. The palms of his hands were always dry, he moved around the house absorbed in thought, rigid somehow, as if his entire body had some other purpose. He was not clumsy: when he picked up a brush and leaned toward a canvas, he would swiftly execute the finest strokes. The energy of each muscle poured into his fingertips.

It was quiet at his place. I would come on the local train on a Friday afternoon and bring food and wine. Piotr lived without money. He picked boletus mushrooms and chantarelles and sold them by the roadside; he chopped wood in exchange for honey, flour or milk. Sometimes he was lucky enough to be commissioned to make furniture. I think his parents were dead. He was very slow, softly spoken and half absent, but that did not bother me. It gave me more breathing space. I was very much in love with Piotr, and I thought of him as my softer, gentler side. When I told him that, he would just laugh. In the evenings sometimes we would drink mulled wine in bed. Then he would lower his wet lips on my skin and in the slow, relaxed way of someone for whom time has no meaning, he would glide them along my neck, over my breasts and down my stomach.

I slept like a baby in his bed. On Saturdays I would be woken up by the smell of his home-baked bread. He would bring me a wooden dish with two huge slices of it, spread with lard and sprinkled with red paprika. We would have the bread and barley coffee for breakfast. In the afternoons we drank Russian tea with vodka. He would paint for a while and I would read him my poems. He was a good listener. He told me that my poetry was good, that it emanated something dark and violent, and painful as well. He would look at me every so often with searching eyes, as if the person reading the poetry was a woman he did not know. When I told him I was going to New York, he said, 'You will be completely different when you come back. You won't need me any more.' I cried. He gave me a list of paints he needed. I bought them as soon as I arrived and mailed them to him. He has probably used them all up by now. Sometimes I can feel myself missing his attentive ear, the way in which he penetrated to the hidden meaning of my words.

When I met José, Piotr turned into a frayed picture in a gold locket, a shooting star which suddenly receded into the night to die somewhere in the distance. Piotr was lost to me. I had lost him and, when I think of it now, I am sorry, because even though I now know that I am condemned to a particular kind of loneliness, I may still be in need of old friends.

I stopped writing when I met José. I did not write poetry or continue my thesis. At first I thought it was because my language was shrinking, retreating into itself, getting too small for me, like a cotton T-shirt soaked in cold water. The words no longer flowed. Some dropped from my vocabulary of their own accord, some I had to think about before I could remember them, and others chafed me, were cumbersome or uncomfortable. Increasingly I experienced language physically, like a tart taste in my mouth as I spoke the words, or like clammy hands as I carefully sifted through the meaning of the English sentences that slid out of my mouth like spaghetti. I noticed that José's body had moved in between me and my text. In my behaviour, in my focus on him and my fear of misunderstanding, I divested myself of everything that might prevent me from getting closer to him, even if it was my own language, and my own text. While José was alive and while we were together, my writing had no importance.

It strikes me that in our everyday lives we use words like frozen food from the supermarket. We defrost them quickly in our mouths and they come out ready to serve. It is only different when I write, because then I pick, prepare and cook them myself. Some I use raw, others I sprinkle on the text like marjoram or pepper, like aromatic spices. José had implanted uncertainty in me, constantly questioning the meaning of the spoken word. It was no longer enough simply to utter the word; it had to be carefully heard in context. It was the same with reading – to read the words inscribed all over the surface of the skin and the body was something else I had to learn, a new kind of concerted attention. Perhaps that was why I could not just tell him to leave me alone, that I wanted to be alone because I wanted to write. All my desires were directed toward, subordinated to, the one desire to be with him, to be together forever. Two naked, smooth souls which at one moment would completely dissolve and become one. I felt that not a single part of me had any autonomy any more. I was without weight, without substance, as if I had been sucked empty. I depended on him, on his desire, touch, chance smile, on the warmth deposited in the small recesses between us. I knew that I did not exist without him.

This morning, as I was wiping the kitchen table, I thought that sometimes the most ordinary objects, like a dish or a knife or a coffee cup, helped me not to lose myself entirely. I was so light, almost non-existent.

VI

I n the middle of November, several things happened at once.

First Inês announced out of the blue that she would be coming to spend a few days with her sisters in San Francisco. The telephone rang in the middle of the night and she simply told him she was coming. José had had no time to prepare himself. I saw the look on his face as he listened to her. It was the look of a man who, with a start, recognized the voice of someone he had lost long ago and who was now calling from God knows where, from some forgotten, completely spent life. Sitting up in bed, he put down the receiver and stared out of the window. I put my arms around him. The blue neon light of the sign on the bookstore glared at us from the building across the way. It was quiet, and I felt that with her every word he was moving away from me, as if he were no longer sitting in bed but in the other corner of the room, as if he would soon disappear from sight altogether. 'I do not want to go back to São Paulo. I do not want to go back to Inês,' he told me. Yet, in spite of his words, that night the future came between us for the first time. The sound of the telephone and Inês's voice cut our common life in half. I suddenly became aware that the future existed, and it was slipping away from me. I slid down under the covers. I thought how this time José had spoken the right words: I do not want. I do not want, I do not want, I do not want. I kept repeating his words to myself, listening to them echoing inside me, falling into my dark, velvety depths. But that night I already sensed that his own desire was too weak to keep him by my side.

That night a crack appeared in the single organism of our bodies.

The next day José left for San Francisco. When we were together, time did not exist. When he left, I felt as if the time we had spent together would fit into the palm of my hand, like a heavy, soggy chunk of bread. I had the feeling that I could break it off the loaf, squeeze it in my fingers for a long time until it turned back into dough, into a ball the size of a marble, which I would then melt in my mouth, slowly and with particular pleasure, the way I used to do under the table at lunch when I was a child. This kind of squeezed time, time reduced to its original form, was gummy and sweet. And although now my memory of all those days together has blended into a single, sticky mixture, I remember the days spent without him very clearly. I see those three days separately, as if they were etched in metal. The edges are so sharp that I feel I could still cut myself on them.

It was a Friday, the first day without him. I awoke feeling that I had been given a present of the day. As I opened the window, the wind rushed in and swept the room of the remains of the night. The sky was cloudless, dazzling bright, like aluminium foil. I thought that it had been days, years, maybe, since I had opened a window like that and looked out into the street, breathing the air into my lungs. The leaves had long since fallen off the stunted birch tree and were lying in small rotting piles on the sidewalk. The man selling hot dogs and pretzels across the street had rolled up the blue canvas awning, and their smell wafted all the way up to the second floor. The wind chased crushed Coca-Cola cans, cardboard boxes and newspapers flapping like wings down the street. The city entered the room and stayed there long after I had closed the window. I took a hot shower, standing there until my skin turned red. Then I made myself a breakfast of toast and cottage cheese. That first morning without José was a day for myself. My very own day.

I decided to tidy up. First I had to clear up all the manuscript pages strewn on the floor by the bed. On top was an ashtray full of cigarette butts. One had fallen out and burned through a few leaves of paper – there was a small brown-edged hole right next to Julia Kristeva's name. Some pages were blotched with coffee stains or glass marks; one had a corner torn off. José had probably jotted down a phone number on it. Incredibly this messy, dusty pile of papers made up the notes for my thesis, written in a minute hand in Polish. I felt with a certain sadness that, like everything else that existed outside of this room, outside of this bed, these notes were a part of me I had long since forsaken. I put the notes away in a folder; thrust in somewhere near the top was a photocopy of George Herbert's poem *Love* (III):

Love bade me welcome yet my soul drew back,
    Guilty of dust and sin.
But quick-eyed Love, observing me grow slack
    From my first entrance in,
Drew nearer to me, sweetly questioning
    If I lacked anything.

'A quest,' I answered, 'worthy to be here':
     Love said, 'You shall be he.'
'I, the unkind, ungrateful? Ah, my dear,
     I cannot look on thee.'
Love took my hand, and smiling did reply,
     'Who made the eyes but I?'

'Truth, Lord: but I have marred them; let my shame
     Go where it doth deserve.'
'And know you not', says Love, 'who bore the blame?'
     'My dear, then I will serve.'
'You must sit down,' says Love, 'and taste my meat.'
     So I did sit and eat.

I read through Herbert's poem perfunctorily at first, and then more carefully, stopping at the last lines. *'You must sit down,' says Love, 'and taste my meat.' So I did sit and eat.*

At that moment I was not aware of the real meaning of Herbert's lines. I felt only the hardness of the paper in my hand and the joyous way the words entered me, as if I were absorbing them so that I could store them in some dark recess of my memory until I needed them again.

My whole day was aglow with this feeling, and I went around town with the joy of a child who has been allowed to go to the movies for the first time on its own. I lunched at the Old Town Bar off Union Square, a student haunt. I ran into Patrick there. 'I've been calling and calling you,' he said. 'At first I thought something was wrong, then that you had left. Finally I realized it must be a man.' There was no point now in trying to explain to him what it was really about: my systematic, deliberate exclusion of the outside world was impossible to explain anyway. I asked if I could meet him the next afternoon. 'I need your help – I'm way behind,' I said, as if that would justify my long absence.

I was not sure why I had invited him; I do not know to this day. Was it because I was alone and afraid of being alone, or in a momentary burst of enthusiasm, did I really plan to make up for lost time with the translations? Patrick rocked back and forth in the chair, his pale blue eyes observing me over the rim of the beer can as he drank it. 'You're not like yourself any more,' he said tersely. That hurt me, I sneaked a quick look at my reflection in the glass behind his back, but said nothing to either confirm or refute his words. Maybe it's already visible, the presence of someone else in my body, on my face, I thought. A heightened, feverish awareness of what was happening inside me was eating away at me, and I could barely manage to think about how my face might look to others. But that was soon corrected, because when I went to the department library, Daisy greeted me by name. 'Hello, Tereza,' she said, and that felt good. I took a new lined yellow notepad out of my bag and worked for two hours; then, for no reason whatsoever, I took myself off to Bloomingdale's. I walked round the cosmetics department the way somebody else would walk around a museum, looking at the Christmas sales, which had already started. Then I went back to the Village. When I passed a Thai restaurant on Second Avenue, the smell of fish was so enticing that I went in and bought some for my supper.

Greeted by an empty apartment, I sat down at the kitchen table and ate the fish. It was completely tasteless, as if it had turned into rubber on the way home. Gazing at the chair where José had sat, I suddenly became afraid that he might not return to New York. This perfidious feeling, which had remained hidden all day long, now emerged and sat there amid the cold remains of the fish on the table, in his empty chair, in the silent kitchen. Still, I found it easier to have this fear out in the open, visible at least, even if it was so horribly slimy. I felt sick. I vomited and immediately felt better for it, as if, along with the fish, I had also thrown up that creeping sense of fear. A sense of peace and absolute certainty had gripped me while I still had my head in the toilet bowl: the separation of the two of us was impossible, it simply could not happen.

I had no reason to think so at the time. I had no plan. The certainty came from the new organism that was me, from the confidence of that new being, which possessed knowledge my old subconscious could not grasp. There was still no sign that José might not return, still no visible threat. But it was present in the apartment, in the air around me, in the feeling of abandonment that took root inside me that evening. It seems quite incredible to me now that I did not notice it immediately, as soon as José decided to go to San Francisco. But even troubled by this sense of undefined danger, I went to sleep that night knowing that somewhere in my veins, in my bones, in my flesh, everything had already been decided. That the future, inasmuch as it existed for us at all, was already here. What had already happened between us, as well as what we were still unaware of and what was yet to happen – that, too, was forever.

The second day also started off in a quiet, relaxed way, although the food I was putting into my mouth still seemed tasteless. The bread was like sawdust, and when I took a bite out of a banana, it smelled of rot. I met up with Patrick at the Italian restaurant on Thirteenth Street, near Seventh Avenue. I am prone to believe that it was out of pure, unbearable loneliness. He immediately observed that I had not invited him to lunch at my place, and took it as a precautionary measure on my part. Since our other lunches had usually ended up in bed, this, he deduced, was meant to show that my body was off limits as far as he was concerned. The pasta, home-made cannelloni, was excellent. We drank some good *vino da tavola*, and that softened the painfully clear message that we were to remain nothing more than friends. But as soon as we arrived at the apartment, Patrick started to behave as if he had never left it. He knew exactly where to find the wine. He opened the first bottle and poured us another glass. I realized that it would be hard to stop him now, and that it was just a matter of time before he would come on to me. To my own surprise, I did not reject the idea – it seemed a technicality somehow, as if it were part of a performance in which I was not really taking part.

I was just afraid to be alone. And perhaps I was curious. When Patrick had rung the bell at the usual time on Friday afternoons, I had simply not opened the door. 'Your lover is coming,' José would say, watching him turn into our street from Second Avenue. He would utter the words with just the faintest trace of irony, which did little to mask his masculine pride. Unlike Patrick, he did not consider himself my lover. In the newly established hierarchy of our vocabulary of intimacy, a lover was someone with a tenuous, temporary status, a person of second-class standing. So, indirectly, our relationship was categorized as definite and strong – institutionalized, even – because José did not have to ring. He had a key to my apartment. Patrick would nervously press the downstairs buzzer, and then step back and look up at the window. 'It's open, I know you're in there.'

'We're different,' José said. 'We are betrothed.' Betrothed? I shuddered slightly at the word, it sounded awkward and saccharine to my ear, Latin-American kitsch. We made love by the window, as if Patrick could see us. José was not particularly inquisitive about my previous lovers, and I was glad, because I did not like talking about them. I was somehow ashamed of my former relationships with men who had scratched the surface of my body, knowing nothing, understanding nothing. I told him about Piotr in his wooden house. Piotr who might still be waiting for me. I had to – he wrote to me regularly in the beginning. I did not answer his letters – did not even open them. It was easier that way. But I mentioned him at the very beginning in an attempt to create a fallback position, as a counterpoint to Inês; to show José that I had somebody too. Yet I already knew how futile and stupid it was to introduce Piotr's name like that. José was too keenly aware of my feelings for him to take any interest in Piotr.

That evening, after a moment's hesitation, Patrick placed his hand on my stomach and then quickly slipped it in between my clothes and my body. 'Not in the kitchen,' I said. He looked at me in surprise, and drew me into the dark narrow front hall. Leaning against the wall, I gave myself to him right there, on my feet. As he was unbuttoning my jeans and pulling them off, I thought of how my surrender to him had been pre-arranged by secret signals, how we had both known that entering the apartment meant entering me. Kneeling down, Patrick lifted my leg over his shoulder. His jabbing tongue was hot. I trembled with excited pleasure, forgetting everything else for a moment, forgetting that it was Patrick. Only the touch mattered to me. But when he closed in, when he finally entered me, something inside me fell flat. His saliva was unexpectedly bitter in my mouth, and the smell of his sweat was alien. I felt the coldness of the wall against my back. I had a sense of having moved so far away from him that I could see both of us standing there in the hall. He penetrated me as if he were searching for something. I heard him say something, cry out. His movements became faster and faster. Then he stopped and, with a long sigh, stood there for a moment, leaning against me. But I was no longer with him, I was somewhere else. I was merely the shadow of the woman in Patrick's arms. My body stayed leaning against the wall for a while, wooden.

Perhaps I needed proof that I could not find pleasure with anyone else. Maybe that was why I gave in to him, let him come into the apartment without a word. I did not feel guilty – I did not feel anything. I was satisfied enough with that.

We fell asleep in each other's arms. As I dozed off I perceived the difference between José and Patrick. It was not just the way they made love: José allowed no void between the two of us. We breathed, murmured, whimpered, moaned, groaned or exchanged short, mangled sentences. When the touching stopped, the silence that sometimes followed was hard to overcome, like a path dusted with white powder which shows up every footprint. The few words we did exchange would cross this space slowly, stumbling like toddlers, not quite sure of their meaning, of whether they would safely reach the person they were intended for. That seemed unimportant compared with the fluent understanding of our bodies. But sometimes, at the beginning, I sensed how hard it was for us to bear that moment of separation and then I would be afraid of losing him. Although that feeling of temporary division almost disappeared later, the danger of it reappearing still remained.

On the day of José's departure for San Francisco, I had again felt a rift opening up between us. At ten minutes past two (I remember the time exactly because he had a four o'clock flight to San Francisco), I stopped a man on the corner of Forty-Fourth Street and Sixth Avenue to ask him the time. With his finger, he lifted back his coat sleeve and, without breaking his stride, said, 'Ten past two.' Good, I thought, we still have time for a cup of coffee. A strong northerly wind was blowing. José, his blue woollen cap pulled down to his eyes, turned to me and said, 'See you in five days.' He said it like the man with the watch, as if he had rolled back an imaginary coat sleeve and thrown out the sentence in passing. It did not matter that I already knew when we would be seeing each other. It was the off-hand way José spoke that shocked me. His words blew away into the winter wind, into the subway railing. They clunked inside me as if they had been dropped into an empty tin can. I could feel the wind filling the sudden void between us, swirling my feelings around like litter in the street.

The sound of José's hollow words returned to me that afternoon, as Patrick curled up against me in his sleep.

It was already dark when I woke up. Patrick was standing in front of one of the enlarged prints of José on the wall. 'You live with him? With this Indian?' he said. His voice was hard and cold, as if he was asking me for some sort of logical explanation, some reason why I had committed this act of betrayal. I looked at Patrick, at his naked body, at his white skin, which looked even whiter in the wake of his words. He stood there pointing at the photograph, waiting for an answer. What could I tell him? That José was no 'Indian'? His parents were as white as Patrick's. That I did not care what colour he was, that I adored the taste of his golden skin, each and every part of it? Or that at this moment I found Patrick's freckled pink whiteness positively disgusting?

I said that was not the point. José and I were both total

90

foreigners lost in the wilderness. We simply belonged to each other. I tried to explain that life with José was not all that simple. 'We quibble over so many things. It's not just the absence of a common language – it's films, the news, the landscape, the bad weather. But I love him. Sometimes he'll say in the street, "This damned winter!" With hate in his voice, as if winter were to blame for something; as if it is intruding between us. I will take his hands, and slip them under my coat to give them some of my warmth. I am cold, too, but I do not hate winter – on the contrary, I love the cold touch of the wind on my face. In the middle of the street we are both on enemy territory, we both have only each other.'

'That's not the same,' Patrick said with unwarranted anger. 'New York is your city just as much as it is mine. It's these South Americans – they're invading us like ants. As if we didn't have enough blacks already. They're inundating us. And there are the Chinese, and the Koreans. This city can't defend itself against them any more. We should throw them all into the sea like rats! I know them, I've sailed the South American coast, on both sides.' Patrick was standing over me as if I were responsible for all the Latinos in New York. 'They're drunks, crooks, animals.' His blue eyes fixed me with their absent stare, as if I could not even imagine how stealthy and dangerous these people living by the river in the dark green shadows of the primeval forest were. As if they were snakes. 'They should be finished off,' he said.

He did not notice the change taking place in him as he talked. All he saw was my body, which now belonged to a savage and had to be punished for it. His eyes were dangerously bright. There was no gentleness or passion in his movements now as he held my arms above my head with one hand and spread my legs open with the other. He rammed himself at me, as if collecting a debt. He deliberately hurt me. I did not defend myself – it was impossible to defend myself against this transformed wild man, against the barrage of blows that pummelled my face, my breasts, my stomach. It struck me that Patrick and I had been speaking Polish all afternoon, even when making love. For all the pain, I felt like laughing at my own crazy faith in the power of words, in the power of speech and in the possibility of communication. All of José's silences, all the hesitations, withdrawals, tremors of uncertainty which would momentarily cloud his face, all the little tiffs – they all seemed so trivial compared with what had happened between us that I started to cry.

Patrick finally stopped hitting me, his fury subsiding as suddenly as it had started. He brought a wet towel from the bathroom and wiped my face, kissing my breasts and stomach, kissing every part of my body which only a minute before he had been battering with his fists. 'Don't cry,' he said. 'Please don't cry. I don't know what got into me.' Then he lay down next to me, talking to me softly, as if I were a child he was rocking to sleep. Maybe he thought I was crying because of him, but all I could think of as his blows rained down on me was José. Words – José's, Patrick's or anybody else's – seemed so meaningless now, like glittering smithereens of broken glass falling all around. José and I could manage without them.

I understood then with all my being that our love was stronger than the two of us, wiser than the two of us, that it embraced us like two halves.

Sometime in the middle of the night the phone rang. I did not pick it up. I lay still on the edge of the bed, laden with pain. Patrick was asleep in the middle of the bed, his back turned to me. Every so often he would wake up, change the compress on my face and bring me a glass of water. The cut on my lip was stinging and my own difficult breathing sounded as if it belonged to someone else. I knew it was José calling. He might have forgotten the time difference between San Francisco and New York, or maybe that was the only time he could call. He had probably waited for the whole house to go to sleep: Felipe, Inês, her two sisters and their husbands. Then he had tiptoed out into the hall and closed the bedroom door behind him, softly, so that it did not squeak. I could see him standing there in the dark, as if I were standing next to him. He let the phone ring for a long time, an eternity, and then broke the connection and tried again. He must have been thinking that I was so sound asleep I did not hear the phone. Perhaps he was struck by a fleeting suspicion that I was not at home at this hour, but he quickly brushed away the thought, as if wiping clean a foggy window with his hand.

I imagined him returning to bed and, awake now, running his had down Inês's body, over her full breasts, softened by the nursing, over her stomach. She turned on to her side in her sleep, nestling up to him, and José was immersed in a pleasant feeling of closeness. Both slept naked, that was their way. Who knows, maybe in São Paulo he used to wake her up on a Sunday morning by gently, carefully, penetrating her sleeping body? He liked the way she wriggled in her sleep, positioning her body in anticipation of pleasure. Inês could cheat on me so easily in her sleep, José might have thought, she wouldn't even know she was doing it. When at last she stirred, they would have to be quiet and make love almost without moving, so as not to wake Felipe. I knew José must have been remembering all this when he returned to bed that night and curled up against Inês's sleeping back. With the touch of her body, he entered his own memory as if he were walking into an open house – but a barely familiar house which both did and did not belong to him.

'I'll make you another baby, and another, and another,' I imagined José whispering into her ear on such a Sunday morning.

That night fear seeped into my thoughts of José. I knew Inês must be telling him the news from São Paulo. She was telling him that his mother was worried because he did not write and that his father's blindness was growing irreparably worse, but that he continued to paint and sometimes, in the early evening, when he was in a good mood, he would dance the waltz with José's mother, just as they used to when they were young. Inês would be telling him that Felipe was getting another tooth – she had discovered it while feeding him with a spoon. I knew that José was sinking into her words as if they were quicksand, and the thought tormented me. As I lay there next to the sleeping Patrick, for the first time I thought of Inês as a real rather than an imaginary danger. She existed. He was with her now. I still did not understand the full meaning of that, but I could feel the blood pounding in my temples as my agitation increased. José already seemed to be on the other side of the abyss, beyond my reach. The embryo of a migraine was lurking somewhere in the back of my head. For the umpteenth time I saw in my mind's eye the lines of his face, the wrinkles around his eyes, his eyebrows, hair and mouth, until finally I felt that he was here, near me. That made me feel a bit better. I knew that, if he really did leave, I would not be able to live without him. I also knew – with my body, not my mind – that would not happen.

I spent almost all of the next day in bed. I woke up around noon. Patrick had just made some coffee, boiled an egg and poured a glass of orange juice. He put it all on a tray and brought it to me in bed. As I drank the orange juice, the cut on my lip began to sting as if someone had held a burning match to it. Patrick said we had to have a serious talk about my life. He invited me to move in with him. We could go away somewhere for Christmas, he said. In the daylight his face looked tired and wan. There were dark circles under his eyes and shaggy strands of reddish hair tumbled over his forehead. His voice was worried and unbearably intimate. 'You're sick, you're falling apart. Don't you see that this guy is driving you to ruin?' he said. I turned my head away. He went on talking, but I was not listening any more. Finally he left. It was early afternoon. He said that he would return in the evening, that I should rest. He did not mention the previous day's incident.

I could hardly wait for him to go, for the grey gaping mouth of day to swallow him up.

I was alone. For the first time since José had left, I felt our physical separation in the form of pure pain. Nothing had prepared me for it. His departure was not the problem – that was something I thought I could bear, at least briefly. The worst thing was that I kept feeling that I wasn't here, in this apartment, in this bed; that I had left with him. That I was in San Francisco, following his every move from within me. I felt a direct connection with him at all times, as if I had moved out of my skin and into his. I was afraid that I was hallucinating. That sometimes happened to me when I was a child. I would suddenly get a headache, lie down and, half asleep, dazed with pain, it was as if I could see pictures from someone else's life, as if I could enter their thoughts. Since I associated these visions with headaches and nausea,

I always tried to forget them, to calm myself down and let the darkness engulf me. As a child, these nightmares scared me, especially as I did not know whether I was simply imagining them or actually seeing them, and I could not talk about it. I was afraid they would say I was crazy. I had a crazy uncle, my father's older brother, who died in a mental hospital before I was born, and terrible stories were told about him: that he was clairvoyant, that he could predict when people would die, that he was kept tied up in a little room. My parents were careful, of course, not to talk about it in front of me. Later, when I reached puberty, the headaches disappeared and returned only when my mother was dying. I tried to forget it all. But that night, before I was fully awake, I recognized the old familiar pain at the back of my head. During the day my headache got worse and spread, leaving just the tiniest passage, a minute opening in my consciousness, for the images to stream in.

I saw that the apartment in San Francisco was full of people. Inês and two of her sisters, Marta and Carolina, were making rice with pork. Felipe was asleep. José was watching TV. Then my eyes followed Inês into the bathroom. She went in, pulled back the plastic blue curtain and turned on the shower. She soaped her body in quick, circular movements, and then stood still, her head slightly raised and eyes closed, letting the water rinse the suds off her face, her stomach and her back. José stepped into the bathroom. She pulled back the curtain. He looked at her as if seeing her for the first time. The sight of her made him unsure of himself somehow. He was on the verge of recognizing some other figure, some other body, other smaller, paler breasts. The spray hitting the plastic curtain pounded louder and louder in his ears, the steam fogged his vision and he was no longer sure who this woman was, standing so still under the shower, waiting. I'm not sure of anything any more, thought José, leaning against the wet tiles. Not for the first time in the previous three days, reality was slipping away from him. He knew only one thing at that moment: he knew that he had to return to New York if he wanted to shake off this feeling of mounting uncertainty. He could feel the faint flutter of his own heart somewhere behind his ribcage. As if I'd swallowed a live bird, thought José as the sweat trickled down his brow.

On the other side of the American continent, in a hollow apartment in New York, loneliness was setting around me like gelatine.

I cannot pinpoint exactly when it fully came to me that I would not let us part. It must have been a gradual thing.

The night before José left for San Francisco, I could not sleep. He had gone to bed early, and I had stayed in the kitchen to wash up. We had had trout and potato salad for dinner and the sink was full of potato peelings, fish guts and the remains of parsley and onion. I sat at the table for a while, filing my nails. I was thinking of nothing, nothing at all. A warm languidness had taken hold of me, as if I were slipping into a warm bath – a feeling I always got when I wanted to escape from reality. Before an exam I used to spend hours sometimes filing my nails, methodically repeating the same action over and over again, like a madwoman.

When I went into the bedroom, José was already asleep. He was lying on his back, legs slightly spread open, the cover pulled down to his waist, arms flung above his head. He was breathing quietly and evenly. I was surprised how peacefully he slept, by the way he surrendered himself so totally to sleep. I do not know why, but I thought it was not good for him to sleep like that, because something could happen to him. It occurred to me for the first time how deadly sleep can be. The thought seemed unwarranted at the time, and shuddering at the idea that I was just as exposed in my own sleep to the whims of chance, I stepped over to the bed. I ran my fingers along José's forehead, face and neck. Then I placed my hand around his throat and began to squeeze, slowly at first, then harder and harder, wondering how long it would take him to wake up. But I suppose I did not squeeze hard enough, because he did not really come to. He merely squirmed, brushed my hands off his neck, and went on sleeping.

Just before that, there was a moment, a crystal-clear moment, when I felt that he was completely in my power. That I could kill him. The vein on his neck began to throb violently under my fingers. It is measuring time, I thought as the glaring streetlight spilled on to his face. I remember the prickly feeling in my fingertips, as if they were the reservoir where my energy was collected and transformed into thin steel knives which threatened to cut into José's flesh.

I think that was when I realized I possessed a terrible power over him – not only the power to change his life, but to take it away completely. José had given me this power himself. I imagined it as the sudden pressure, the firm squeeze that took his breath away and completely paralyzed him at the same time. That night I felt that I was holding José's soul in my hands.

I will never give it back to you, never, and you will never give mine back to me, I thought, and let him sleep.

The other important event before Christmas was the letter from Uruguay. I took it from José's pigeonhole at school the day he left. I knew he had been waiting for it impatiently. José had been in touch before with some of the sixteen survivors of the crash in the Andes and it had been hard for him to persuade them to try again to recall their time in the mountains when, in order to survive, they had had to eat human flesh. I think what interested him most was their feeling for God, and the fact that the Catholic Church had never officially condemned cannibalism. The Bishop of Montevideo, however, had refused to recognize the act of the survivors as a representation of holy communion, and this deeply offended some of them. According to what José had told me, the man whose letter he was expecting had played a pivotal role in the group's survival. When they had had to make their decision, it was Pedro Algorte who uttered the key words. He said: 'This is like holy communion.' He also told them that Christ had given his body in death for them to live spiritually, and that their friends were now giving their bodies for them to live physically. Most of the young men were strong Catholics and this idea, they later declared, helped them to overcome their moral crisis and do the only thing they could do to stay alive. José thought it had all been quite simple until then. Not only the Uruguayan Catholic Church, but even the Vatican itself, confirmed that the young men had been right and that their decision had been ethical. Later, however, some of the survivors started publicly insisting that this act had been equal to holy communion. The Catholic Church refuted their claim. I think José was planning to include this debate in this book, along with some of the letters of those who died, who confirmed therein that once dead, they were willing to offer themselves as food for their comrades so that the others could survive.

The address on the blue envelope had been written in

green ink, in a small, gentle, almost feminine hand. The same person had added the name of the sender. The seal on the envelope was already broken, and it looked to me as if someone had opened it before me and then tried to seal it again, not very successfully. Perhaps the sender had had second thoughts. With the fastened envelope flap still wet and the sweet taste of glue still on his tongue, he had suddenly changed his mind. Carefully, he re-opened the envelope and took out the letter to add something important. Holding the letter in my hand, I felt that I could see him, this unknown man with opaque eyes betraying no emotion, sitting in his office in Montevideo, thoughtfully putting the letter to one side on his desk. He probably hesitated, thinking that the few words he had suddenly remembered would not change anything anyway. And then, as always when he remembered the mountains, a profound sadness must have washed over him. The many years that had passed since the plane crash meant absolutely nothing to him, because all the faces and events were firmly fixed in his mind as vividly as ever. Even now, by a special trick of the memory, he could transport himself on to the slopes of the Andes. The worst thing was that there was no forgetting, and this was something you could not explain to anyone, thought Pedro Algorte, fingering the envelope and the top and the edge of his desk, like a blind man. Perhaps he was telling himself again that his conscience was perfectly clear, that he was at peace with the world and with God and, in the final analysis, with himself. But there was no forgetting. Not even in his sleep. Sometimes he dreamed of golden yellow oranges floating above him. He wanted to reach for them, but something was pressing down on his arm. He would look and see that it was snow. Snow like stacked rocks. Meanwhile, the oranges were drifting away. He would never catch them, Algorte knew in his dream. He would wake up screaming, as he had then, and in horror throw the white sheet off his body. They say that during those first days he lost his memory. He did not remember a thing. At least, it looked like amnesia. He had seen the face of death. The face of death was white. And he knew that when it came back for him again, he would recognize that face.

I opened the envelope for no particular reason. Inside were two thin, closely written sheets of paper and several newspaper clippings. Judging by the names mentioned, Algorte was referring José to certain books and to his own correspondence with Monsignor Andres Rubio, who had been Bishop of Montevideo at the time. Also enclosed was a photocopied interview in English, in which the Bishop said that to eat someone who has died is to incorporate his being into yours and can be compared with the transplantation of an organ, the heart or an eye, for instance, into another person. I thought the Bishop had certainly not mentioned the eye and the heart by chance, although the question of whether the recipients of the organ actually felt themselves to be 'incorporating' another being remained unanswered. We had discussed it once, and José had said that the recipient felt nothing, that he simply forgot about it after a while. I thought it surely could not be quite as simple as that, especially not for people who were religious. I wondered whether they found justifications similar to those of the young men in the Andes. Algorte was obviously quoting certain people from the Vatican, as well as the Jesuit Richard McCormick. The envelope also contained a photocopy of a letter from Gustav Nicholich, one of the young men who had died. It was a long letter, but I think I recognized a quotation, because

José, fascinated by it, had translated it into English for me. 'I came to the conclusion that the bodies are here because God put them here and, since only the soul matters, I need not have a guilty conscience; if the day comes when I too can save someone with my body, I will gladly agree to it.'

Holding the letter in my hand, it never occurred to me how odd it was that I remembered those particular words.

VII

Four days of physical work had left me exhausted. I did not feel well. I was tired not only because of the amount of work I had done but also because of all the unnecessary energy I had put into it, as if by scrubbing the tiles or the floor as hard as I could I was trying to prove something to myself. Perhaps my own existence. I had to slow down and rest, but I felt like a programmed machine which will not switch off until it finishes the job it has started. The apartment was not yet completely clean, and there were still the last remains of the body waiting to be deposited somewhere across the river. My hands shook with fatigue as I washed the dishes, and a wine glass dropped on the floor and broke.

They were our favourite glasses – crystal with a gold border. The woman we had bought them from at the fair claimed they were the last ones left from her grandmother's wedding set, and told us she was selling them reluctantly. I believed her, and it made me feel bad. When we brought them home I felt as if we had taken a piece of somebody else's past in order to move into our own present. We should have bought everything new, things without a past. But the few possessions which had helped us gain a better foothold in the material world had become meaningless now, anyway. The material world had shattered into smithereens without José, and it was all the same to me if tomorrow someone else would be using our cups, our remaining glasses, plates or spoons. Putting the clean dishes away in the cupboard, I touched them with disgust, as if the green mould of oblivion had already started to spread over them.

I was grateful to José for having seen to his own clothes. It would have been too much for me to have had to dispose of them as well. I had enough things to do as it was, because apart from the cleaning, every night I had to carry these cumbersome and anything-but-light packages to different parts of New York. Otherwise the smell of decaying flesh would have become unbearable. The bathroom already had a persistent odour to it, which came from the drain. When I opened the door, it was like being knocked back by the stench of Warsaw's dirty, half-empty butchers' shops, the stench that comes from entrails, from rotting pieces of meat which already look gangrenous. My hair, too, must have absorbed the smell, like fabric. I was going to have to keep washing it until I completely got rid of the unpleasant stink.

My whole body still trembles at the thought of all the effort that went into putting everything in order. I never thought it would be easy to carry out the decision once I had made it, but I had not known how much strength it would require, how much plain physical strength and stamina. Sometimes I would collapse in the middle of the job. If only I could have, I would have had a long, dreamless sleep.

*

What do people think of when they talk about their lives? Do they really see them as an integral whole, as a chronological sequence of events; as something logical, purposeful, completed? What moments do they remember, and how do they remember them? As words? As a series of images and sounds? My life crumbles into a series of pictures, unconnected scenes which come to mind only occasionally and at random. But there are key events, the acts of chance or fate, which later enable me to construct a logical whole of my life. One such moment was meeting José. The other was my decision to see our love through to the very end.

It was made in the three days I spent without him, the only three days we were apart, though I was not immediately conscious of my choice then. That was when the resolution took root and matured. A few elements were still missing, but my later trip to San Francisco, our talks, his hesitation, simply reinforced my conviction that we could not separate, that it was not an option. There was no going back to our old lives. In the three days that I was alone in New York while José was in San Francisco, it became strikingly clear to me that not only was the future a threat to us, but the past too had started to come between us. All I knew was that I had to be strong for both of us if I wanted to preserve our love.

José did not talk about returning to São Paulo. 'Departure' was too enormous and heavy a word for either one of us to utter. But even left unsaid, it cast a menacing shadow over us. Only that once, after being summoned to San Francisco, did he say that he did not want to go back to South America. I pretended not to hear, as if he had not been talking to me. It was enough for me to know what he thought on the subject. On the other hand, I knew that contemplation of the past was like a cracked vessel leaking water. At first all you see is the wet stain, then it spreads as the water comes through faster and faster. I was afraid that the past would wash us away. I felt that it was separating us and that soon we would start to forget the most important thing, which was that we could survive only in the here and now. Not in cities like Warsaw or São Paulo, only in New York, which contained us like a huge dirty bowl.

Until José left for San Francisco, I did not think about this all that much. But with him gone, it was as if he had returned to Brazil already. It wasn't that Inês and Felipe had ceased to exist while we lived together, but they had existed in some other invisible layer of foggy reality. The moment his plane took off, the two of them surfaced in my mind, like ships emerging from the mist, threatening to sink me.

On the afternoon of the fourth day I flew to San Francisco. José had phoned in the morning. The conversation had been brief. 'Are you all right?' he had asked, as if sensing something in my voice, deadened by loneliness and his absence. 'No,' I said. 'I am not all right. I'm coming.' Silence. He did not say come. He did not say don't come. He knew it was not up to him. He simply said he would wait for me at a hotel in the centre of town.

It was dusk when I arrived. Through the hotel lobby window I saw José coming down the street. The sky was dark; only the edge along the roofs was still a light colour. He walked as if guarding himself against something, shoulders hunched over, hands jammed deep into his coat pockets. He kept his eyes on the toes of his shoes and the sidewalk, on which the stains of night were beginning to appear. He looked unsure of himself and completely withdrawn, as if he wished that he were not there, that he did not exist. I picked him out of the crowd with my straining eyes. For a moment I was frightened by the crazy accuracy with which I had singled him out, by the dangerous exclusivity which recognized only him, wanted only him and could think of him only as a part of myself. It was like a film in slow motion, I remember with a sharp clarity his every movement, the lost expression on his face, the quiver of uncertainty when he did not see me as soon as he walked through the door. With each step he took, the crystals of desire multiplied inside me. I wanted him at that moment with every part of my body. He turned around, recognized me and took several steps toward me. I wanted to wait nonchalantly in the armchair for him to come over, but I got up and walked toward him. The power of his presence bested my desire to feign restraint. I pressed my cheek against his, cold from the wind borne in from the sea.

How I needed that rough touch of his face and the casual kiss on the head.

I did not want to lose him.

We drank wine in the hotel bar and José, as always, jiggled his leg under the table and chain-smoked. We hardly exchanged a word. After Inês's visit we both seemed afraid to talk. It was impossible to talk about what existed around us. The membrane would disappear, leaving our love naked and unprotected. If that happens, I thought, if he lets Inês and Felipe in now, it will destroy us.

'The day after tomorrow we'll go back to New York together. We'll go home,' José said, looking at me with a smile.

'Yes, home,' I said.

Later, José did not accompany me to my hotel room.

We both knew that we could not be together here in the same way we were in New York. I stayed in the hotel and he returned to his wife. I realized that I was now cast in the mistress's role.

That night I could not get to sleep. Just before dawn I felt a strong urge to go to the house in Steiner Street. Maybe I can catch a glimpse of him, I thought; maybe I can finally see him in his other life – walking by the window holding his child in his arms. He had told me he was not getting any sleep because the baby was keeping him awake at night. Perhaps I would see the child's exhausted face resting on his shoulder. How soothing that touch must be. Perhaps I would see him pacing the room until the child fell fast asleep. Then he would open the window, light up a cigarette and stand there for a while, inhaling the night air in the dead street. If he were by any chance to glance at the shadowy doorway across the way, I would quickly step back into the darkness. But when José closed the window it would feel like a slap in the face.

This daydreaming made me realize that my suffering over being separated from José was quite physical. The headache which had been simmering for two days struck late in the evening and by dawn it had become unbearable. I started to throw up. I never made it to the bathroom – the vomit came spewing out on the bed, the covers, the pillow. In the end I had nowhere to lie except on the floor. Day was already breaking and in the pale light of morning I watched the balls of dust under the bed roll away from my breath. I remembered the photograph of Inês and the baby that José had shown me, the one in which you could not see her face. Suddenly the photograph came alive. Inês raised her head, threw back her hair and finally I saw her face, her dark eyes, thick eyebrows and protruding, almost swollen lips. She was looking at me. Then I knew that she knew about me, and I felt better. The pain in my head immediately eased.

I fell asleep with her gaze on my face.

I do not know whether José told her about me. I don't think so. But there are many indirect ways for a woman to detect in a man's behaviour the presence of another woman. The distracted way he watches television, the attention with which he dresses, the telephone calls where his answers are confined to yes-and-no monosyllables, the searching look he gives his wife when he thinks she is not watching, the air of false conviviality at Sunday lunch. Then there is the amiableness, the exaggerated niceness to the children, the dog, the neighbours. The existence of another woman can also be betrayed in the way he makes love to his wife with fresh passion, as if she has suddenly become another woman herself.

Lying there in the hotel room, knocked out by the migraine, I could imagine the two of them sitting in the deserted kitchen that evening.

She closes the door so that their conversation does not disturb the rest of the household, who have gone to bed, and she waits. He starts by talking at length about his book, knowing it does not interest her in the least. All the same, Inês listens attentively. Sipping her red wine and concealing her impatience, she waits for José to say something about himself, about the two of them. José notices her tension, that fear of the unsaid, but he cannot help her. She asks him nothing, however; not why he has moved out of the university rooms, or where he has moved to. If she did ask him, he might say that the apartment was more convenient, that he had more space, that he shared it with a colleague from the university, or something like that. He would have to lie. She senses this and does not want him subjected to the humiliation of his own lies. So Inês is silent and waits.

I think she must have known what was going on even before this. She must have recognized the telltale signs – the silences, the withdrawal, the distancing. She must also have sensed that it was serious this time. José's thoughts were elsewhere. For the first time he's not here with me, he's there with her, Inês might have been thinking as she watched him searchingly, listening to the tone of his voice to see whether it would reveal the cause of his deep agitation. She looked at his face, at his hands. The boy looks so much like him, she thought, and the thought made her sad. She had had to put up with all those times when he moved away from her for a while. Until now, she had always thought of his adventures like an outbreak of the measles. First there was the incubation period, then the illness would suddenly appear, last for a defined length of time, and then disappear without a trace. 'Men are like children. You don't realize it until it's too late, and in the meantime you suffer,' her mother had told her when she had heard about Consuelo. Her father had not been much better. He had even been known to bring a mistress home to Sunday lunch. 'I don't know of a single man who has not had a mistress, but he always comes back,' her mother would say.

Yes, the majority come back to their wives, but this time Inês was not so sure. The fact was that José's previous mistresses had always been visible. They would surface very quickly in conversation. This time Inês could only guess at the existence of another woman. She was surrounded by a wall of silence from José. It's good that I came, she must have thought. She did not have to ask him anything – José knew that she knew. She knew that he knew that she knew. Inês and José were always playing this game.

110

I am sure that at that moment, José, sitting in the kitchen, still did not know the real reason why Inês had come to San Francisco. Maybe he thought she was just being impulsive as usual, spending money unnecessarily. He did not know that her mother had paid for the trip this time and that visiting her sisters had simply been an excuse to see him. Inês had told her mother that José had seldom called home since he left on his grant, and that when he did he sounded strange and distracted. She also told her that she was expecting their second child. That was enough: her mother understood everything. Inês calculated that once she confronted him with her pregnancy, José would realize that he had to come back to São Paulo and that his life in New York with that woman was over.

On my second day in San Francisco I woke up around noon with my headache gone and feeling quite refreshed. Even without firm proof, I was positive that Inês knew I existed. All decisions concerning José's life were in our hands alone, hers and mine. I still did not know the real reason for her visit, but I sensed I might soon have to do something. Nothing would ever be quite the same between José and I again. His past life, his family, would fester like a tumour and occupy more and more space between us until finally they separated us completely. I stood on the balcony facing south. It was, I remember, a mild, drizzly day. It reminded me of the small French seaside towns where we sometimes used to spend a week or two. My mother was fond of those autumn holidays. The families had gone by then, the sand was damp and heavy and the sea was choppy. There was a constant wind blowing, just as there was here. I looked out toward the houses in Steiner Street. The city looked unreal. The skyscrapers on the horizon resembled children's drawings impaled in the ground. The only activity was in front of the hotel: a dog trotting across the street, a woman opening a garage door and baring her thigh in the process. The aroma of pancakes. Standing on the balcony that day, breathing in San Francisco, I once again felt the abyss opening up before me. I could lose him, I thought as I saw myself tumbling into it.

Finally, José phoned. He sounded panicky. There was no way we could see each other today. We would be travelling back to New York together in the morning anyway. I understood, or at least I tried to understand, even though every postponement heightened my physical need for him. I spent the afternoon in bed, weak, unable to stroll around the city like a tourist. San Francisco throbbed through the closed blinds, but a cobweb of paralyzing fear stretched out between me and reality.

That evening I set out, no longer just in my mind, for the house in Steiner Street, where Inês's sisters lived.

It was not late when I climbed up the hill, around ten o'clock. The dark blue sky hemmed in the black, spiky trees of the nearby park. I took a deep breath and walked toward number 25. It was a quiet, peaceful evening, as if everyone had long since gone to bed. I should turn back, I thought. What if José appears right now? What if he steps out of a taxi or opens the front door of the house and sees me standing there on the sidewalk like a spy? But the street was still, not a single car drove by, not even a dry leaf rustled on the sidewalk. The ground floor was dark. So was the first floor. The entire second floor was ablaze with light. I heard voices and laughter, as if they were having a celebration. Everyone was probably up there, the whole family, friends. José, too, was there, in the womb of this yellow house on Steiner Street, submerged in the velvet of

112

the Portuguese language, seduced by the familiar faces and their warm smiles.

If I could have been sure that Inês was alone that evening, I might have decided to go in. The urge to go up and ring the bell was so strong that I could already feel the pleasant touch of the wooden banister under my fingers. A second before the bell sounded its metallic ring at the door, I might wonder why Inês in particular was his wife, and why she always waited for him so patiently, as if she had all the time in the world at her disposal. Then the door would open and her face would appear. Inês would look at me in surprise, suspiciously, maybe only quizzically. I would finally see this petite woman with her loose brown hair, dressed in T-shirt and trousers, and notice the fragility suggested by her almost childlike figure. I would also see that there was no answer to why it was she who was his wife, that that was impossible to know. Perhaps Inês would gather from some gesture of mine, or from the way I stubbornly stood at the door and showed no intention of leaving, that I wanted to talk to her, and that the matter was urgent. She would step back from the door and let me into the illuminated apartment, which would immediately seem smaller and less bright. She would invite me to sit down, pour me a glass of wine, maybe, and wait.

What would I say to her?

Had I really met Inês that evening, I would have told her that it was impossible for me to part with José. I don't doubt your need to take him back to São Paulo, I would tell her, calling her by her first name, because surely the fact that we were two women tied to the same man automatically implied a certain level of communication, a certain intimacy. But your need for him is different from mine. They are two incomparable types of relationship. You want a normal life with him, you want the child to have a father who will play soccer with him and attend parents' evenings. I want absolute union with him. My love is stronger than I am, than both him and me. It will overcome him, and me and you and the child. It is implanted in my body, and has nothing to do with reason.

I would tell her something else that sometimes troubled me. It was more of an intellectual problem than a real one: I barely dared admit to myself how little I really knew about José. That was part of our tacit agreement: not to ask any questions so that we would not know too much. The truth is that we had only the most general picture of each other. We had only fragmentary facts about each other's education, tastes, political leanings and the books we had read. None of which necessarily made for a meaningful picture of the other. But that did not stop us from being close. I would go so far as to say that it had no effect at all on the way we were together. From time to time, the odd fact would come out and we would not know what to do with it. Sometimes I would wake up thinking that lying next to such a foreigner scared the daylights out of me. But the touch of his skin would sweep away all my doubts, and I would know that in his touch was everything, absolutely everything.

That evening I would have told Inês that I had been taught to expect from a man a relationship based on intel-lectual compatibility, on some degree of understanding and, if possible, on attuned bodies. This was what people got married for, only to become unhappy. Their unhappi-ness was etched in the wrinkles around their mouths and on their foreheads, it could be smelled in their doleful apartments full of books both of them had read and in the dust that had accumulated on them. After graduating from university I lived for three years with a teaching fellow in the department of world literature. He was ten years older than me and divorced. He got me to do a Ph.D., he encouraged me to write poetry. We both cultivated understanding – carefully, considerately, as was expected of people like us. But soon I began to cultivate a hatred as well. That quiet, perfidious, very dangerous kind of hatred which is almost never released in an argument or fight. The relationship simply breaks up and everyone wonders why. I hated him when I realized that he was stringing me along with words. He had an explanation and an argument for everything, even for his own worst behaviour. He was unfeeling, but he concealed it with eloquence and glibness: he existed only in words.

I would tell Inês that our understanding, José's and mine, went deeper than language. Not everything could be said. Not everything should be said. With him I had learned that words were like sea shells – they consisted of hard layers and soft, of an outside and an inside. Our understanding lay in a place that usually eluded language, even at its softest core. It was in this absence of speech that our bodies had assumed the function of communication.

Had I entered the apartment in Steiner Street that evening, maybe Inês would have understood something of what I wanted to tell her. Perhaps she would have leaned toward me, touched my hand or poured another drink. Who knows, maybe she would have told me that she wanted José to go and leave her alone? She had had enough of waiting – it made a person bitter. I am tired, I am so tired, perhaps she would have said, leaning her head on my shoulder as if I could bring her salvation.

But nothing happened. I stood across from number 25 for a while, watching the bright windows, and then I took a cab back to my hotel. I could think only of Inês, as if I had completely forgotten José. One minute I thought of her as an enemy, trying to predict her next move by putting myself in her position. The next I wanted to make friends with her, to learn things about José which I knew I could never learn in any other way.

I could not get warm in bed for ages. The sheets were cold, as if sprinkled with frost. I did not have the strength to think about José, about how he was lying in bed next to Inês now, snuggling up to her, touching her, recognizing her with his hands, his mouth, his body. I was not jealous. He did not belong to her in the way he belonged to me. I fell asleep thinking that all I could hope for was that José, before dozing off, would feel an emptiness inside him. As if he had spent those three days with a stranger, not with his own wife.

In the cab taking me to the airport in the morning, I felt a vague discomfort again. This new force had come between us, Inês's willpower, her determination to take him back to São Paulo. I felt it physically, like tension, anticipation, a stomach-ache, a fever and inner trembling. Now, after my visit to San Francisco, the fear was even clearer. It had assumed a shape. I realized that the fear was of José, not Inês. Until then I had believed we were equal in our search for a solution, but at last I had seen for myself that José was weak and that I could not count on him. He was unable to make any decisions himself. I could count only on him accepting whatever decision I made, and not fighting it.

I also realised that I did not have much time left. The grey winter day hung over the highway like a billowing tarpaulin and the world seemed to be weighing down on me menacingly.

José was already waiting for me at the door of the airport terminal. His skin was grey from sleepless nights, and his kiss was as tender as if it was his last. He is saying goodbye, I thought, but it was not his departure I was thinking of, it was his death. That morning, for the first time, I saw death in his eyes.

'Inês is expecting another child.'

He told me without preamble, while the aircraft sailed across the blueness of the sky. He said it as if reciting a foreign text he had learned. His voice was monotone, like the recorded voice explaining what to do in the event of a forced landing. Now that I think about it, I wonder why he told me on the plane. How was I supposed to react to such news, at an altitude of ten thousand metres, with a cracker in one hand and a watery coffee in the other? I remember the cracker extremely well. It was thin, round and very salty. I still remember the taste of salt on my palate, because at that moment I wished that it were the last bite I would ever take. I wished the plane would crash. If the plane crashed, we would die together and that would be the end of it. What is more, it would have been the last opportunity for us to go to our deaths together. But the plane continued its flight to New York, and as I swallowed the dry cracker, I quickly calculated that we had less than a month left.

Then the feeling I had experienced in the taxi that morning, of the world closing in on me, become clear. It was the image you see on a crashing plane: reality comes at you and you know it is the last thing you will see. Our world was crumbling. The end was inevitable, and it was near. Anyone else might have envisaged various possibilities for us to live together. We could both live in São Paulo or Warsaw, or perhaps even stay in New York. José could leave

Inês and visit the children periodically. We would spend our summers with them. In time Inês would reconcile herself to the situation, perhaps even remarry. But there were reasons why these options were impossible. First of all, José was emotionally spent, as if suddenly he could bear neither the burden of our love nor the loss of it.

José sat for the rest of the trip with his eyes closed, as if he were asleep and quite beyond my reach. He was still with Inês. I knew that's where he was. He was looking at her stomach in disbelief, though nothing showed yet. She had walked him to the door with that serenity so unique to pregnant women. Inês was absolutely sure that he would soon be back, that he would be in São Paulo by Christmas. Whatever happened in the meantime would sink under the weight of her expanding belly. She kissed him on the cheek, and José recognized the smell of Felipe. He felt so faint he wished he could go straight to sleep and never wake up again.

VIII

Emptying the ashtray into the garbage this morning, that word came back to me again: murderer. Like a slap in the face. All day it had left me alone – I had not thought of it once – only to lurch out at me while I was throwing out his cigarette butts. If I had really wanted to kill somebody, it would have been Inês. She was the logical choice. That murder would have had an obvious motive: jealousy. Despite the shock it would cause, everybody would understand the reasons for it. But most motives are false, invented by the police to make it easier for them to classify and close a case. Real motives are unexplainable because they are irrational. Often murders seem to have been planned, with a perfectly rational motive, and then it turns out that people kill each other because it is too hot, or because they don't like the way somebody is looking at them. It had not occurred to me at all to kill Inês. Despite everything, she was a bit-part player. In any case, her death would not have resolved my basic problem, which was how to achieve absolute union with José.

Once we got back to New York, on the surface it was as if nothing had changed. We both behaved that way deliberately, except that I started ticking off the days we had left together. We knew from the very beginning, of course, when our grants would expire and how long I had the rented apartment for. But we never thought about it in terms of how long we had together. When we met, we never dreamed it might be forever. We existed outside time, cocooned in the body, in emotions.

When we returned from San Francisco, we entered the hourglass zone. I could feel every grain of sand trickling from one section into the other, as if I had turned into a time-measuring device myself.

José did not mention Inês anymore, or talk about going back. That was strange, considering how little time we had left, but I understood completely. It was not something that could be talked about, because there was nothing to say. He would undoubtedly repeat that he did not want to go back to São Paulo, even though in a corner of his mind he was there already. But despite our pretence that all was well, José started behaving differently, and I noticed it. As if he had suddenly snapped out of a daze, he started spending more and more hours in the library, trying to make up for lost time. In the evenings he worked on his notes. He did not go to bed at the same time as I did any more. As he sat in the living room, engrossed in his books, I felt a wall going up between us. The changes were tiny, barely perceptible, and only I could have noticed them, but they upset the balance of our relationship.

Fortunately, his attempt to come to his senses did not last long.

Pedro Algorte's letter, which had arrived while José was away, lay on his desk unopened for days, as though he had not even noticed it. He finally picked it up one cold, gusty evening. The wind crept under the window into the room.

It was the first evening we had spent together at home and alone since our return. He was sitting on the couch and I was lying down with my head in his lap. I can remember every detail, as if the position of my body, the taste of my drink, the cold in the tips of my toes, the billowing of the curtain were all significant to what was to come. Like those long descriptions of an interior which set the mood for the main character in a novel, or the descriptions in detective stories where particular details offer the key to solving the crime.

I was holding a gold-rimmed glass of red wine. José, sipping from his own glass, was reading Pedro Algorte's letter. He said nothing, but I could see from his face that its contents were very important to him.

Then he put it aside. 'What perplexes me about those survivors in the Andes,' he said to me, 'is the simplicity of their faith in God. As if up there in those heights there were no obstacles between them and God. The moment they believed that God wanted them to stay alive by eating the corpses of their friends, it all became so simple. They were so close to Him.' José's voice had a tone of envy I had never noticed before.

I listened to him carefully. He was talking about the letter, but he seemed to be talking about something else as well, something he could not fully articulate. He reached for the book *Alive*, which was lying close by, and began to read to me aloud:

Most of the bodies were covered by snow, but the buttocks of one protruded a few yards from the plane. With no exchange of words Canessa knelt, bared the skin, and cut into the flesh with a piece of broken glass. It was frozen hard and difficult to cut, but he

persisted until he had cut away twenty slivers the size
of matchsticks. He then stood up, went back to the
plane, and placed them on the roof. Inside there was
silence. The boys cowered in the Fairchild. Canessa
told them that the meat was there on the roof, drying
in the sun, and that those who wished to do so should
come out and eat it. No one came, and again Canessa
took it upon himself to prove his resolution. He
prayed to God to help him do what he knew to be
right and then took a piece of meat in his hand. He
hesitated. Even with his mind so firmly made up, the
horror of the act paralysed him. His hand would neither rise to his mouth nor fall to his side while the
revulsion which possessed him struggled with his stub-
born will. The will prevailed. The hand rose and
pushed the meat into his mouth. He swallowed it. He
felt triumphant. His conscience had overcome a prim-
itive, irrational taboo. He was going to survive.

'You understand?' José asked.
'I understand,' I said.
And it was true. I could easily imagine the piece of
human meat, no bigger than a matchstick, sliding down
Canessa's throat. I could also imagine the moment when,
transformed by faith, it ceased to be human flesh and
became food, just food which would allow them to survive.
At that moment, as in some kind of ritual, the human flesh
simply became the host. I could imagine it all that evening,
as I watched my glass of wine, bathed in the light, become
paler, like blood. And I could not see why the Bishop of
Montevideo did not understand the point. Even José did
not get it. When I took a sip from my glass it still had the
familiar taste of wine, but at that moment it just as easily

could have been blood. I knew that I would be able to sip blood just as calmly. The idea did not horrify me. I never felt the power of faith as clearly as I did that night. 'Everything is so simple,' I said. 'I'm sure I would have done the same thing in their place. What about you, would you be able to eat human flesh?' I asked José. The lamplight divided his face into two halves, one dark, the other light. There was a long silence.

'If I strongly believed in God, I think I might be able to do it,' he said.

As usual, I watched his face closely, his expressions, his posture, his hands, hoping to find the soft hidden meaning inside the hard armour of his words. José felt my tense exploration of his face, the feverishness of my gaze. Perhaps he sensed that his answer was unusually important to me, crucial, even. The wind was still whistling outside, icy knives stabbed our backs. I kept looking at him, waiting. He seemed to hesitate, to be on the verge of saying something else, something that was gathering in his throat, in his lungs, rising to his lips. But he did not say it. I saw that he had no strength for words other than those he had already uttered. 'I think I could,' he repeated thoughtfully. It was enough for me to imagine him standing in the snow, squinting indecisively, to realize that he would go back to the plane to die rather than eat human flesh. That evening I understood what I had already suspected for some time: that José would have been one of those who had not survived. There were too many maybes in his words, too much hesitation and indecision in his gestures. That evening I sensed that his weakness came from within, that it sprang from his very self, and that therein lay his fate.

*

There are days when you feel that your whole being is cracking apart and suddenly everything becomes different. About ten years ago I was walking my poodle Piko in the park. He was old already, over thirteen and soon afterwards he died. I had known him all his life, inasmuch as one can ever know a dog, and I was prepared to swear that he was a peaceable, loving and harmless animal. But something unexpected happened in the park that day. The only strollers that morning, apart from Piko and me, were a man and a toddler. As we passed each other the little boy made a sudden movement with his arm and the dog went for his leg. The child screamed, his thin, long howl piercing the air. The father turned white with anger but immediately calmed down when he saw that it was not a bad bite. The dog had merely nicked the child with his one and only tooth. There was a trickle of blood which quickly coagulated. But I was shocked. I was shocked by the fact that my dog had done something which so jarred with the picture I had had of him for thirteen years. That day in the park I heard something crack inside me, as if I had suddenly stepped on a thin, dry twig. In the absolute silence around me, this inner explosion reverberated like a gunshot and the world suddenly took on a different colour, the colour of veiled horror. When the boy and his father moved away, I broke into such sobs that Piko started to whimper anxiously. Suddenly nothing was the same any more, the world had lost its footing. I think what upset me most at the time was the very possibility of instantaneous change, the arbitrariness of reality.

That evening, in the wake of José's words, I heard that same inner shattering sound again, like thin glass plates cracking.

Thinking that the subject interested me, José wanted to

translate an excerpt from a book, *O Canibalismo Amoroso*, for me, but I was not in the mood to hear about '*the impulse to incorporate the object of desire*' as expressed in poetic metaphors about rotten fruit and worms. The book was a Freudian interpretation of works from the history of literature, mostly poetry, but such analyses left me cold. However, the engraving on the jacket of the book did catch my eye. It was by Theodor de Bry, and not dissimilar to Johann Froschauer's woodcut at the exhibition where José and I had met. It depicted a man being eaten by Indians. These Indians had better table manners than Froschauer's. They were eating out of dishes. A head was in one bowl, the intestines in another, and the third was already empty. On closer inspection I saw that the engraving depicted only women and children; a dozen naked women with waist-length braids and children hungrily milling around them. I held the book in my hands and stared for a long time at the title page, at these women amusing themselves with food. The title, 'Amorous Cannibalism', coupled with the engraving, seemed to have a special importance. Why were there only women in the picture? It took a while for me to unravel its true meaning.

Over the past three days, having done the unavoidable, I have been trying to remember exactly when it was that I realized that the solution to our relationship was death. José's death, to be precise. I recalled every moment we spent together, as if that could make the decision any easier for me. I did not look for an explanation, because the logic of my own actions was perfectly clear to me. But it was hard.

The problem is what to call it. It is a problem I feel even now, even in my own language. But my time with José made me over-sensitive to words. I think the word 'death' is totally inappropriate for the experience of absolute union between two beings, for the merging of body and spirit. Once I had decided that death was a necessary transitional stage for us to achieve union, I could not accept that José was a mere victim.

His death – and I use the word only as a maladroit technical term – offered us the only possibility of staying together forever. The more I think about it, the clearer it is to me that I reached the decision gradually, very slowly, in fact. Judging by some of the signs, I would say that the same solution might even have occurred to José. He would look at me strangely sometimes, especially when he thought I was preoccupied and did not notice. It was a look I did not know, it came from the corners of his eyes, under half-closed lids, a stalking look which gave me an uneasy feeling; a look in which I was not alive any more. In my mind I called it a deadly look, but I said nothing to José. Fear is not the right word for all the conflicting emotions I felt. I was afraid – afraid of separation, not of physical assault. Had he at any moment come up to me with a knife in his hand, I would not have said a word. I do not think I would even have defended myself. I think I would have stood there quite calmly, because I never saw anything he did as violent.

I did not start planning José's death as soon as we returned from San Francisco. It took me some time to see for myself that he really was fading, disappearing. It was like holding a melting snowball in your hand until all that is left is a wet pool. There was no way I could stop the melting. In the previous few days he had become fidgety, nervous. He would clench his fists on the table in front of him or on his knees, as if pulling at something. He did not seem quite in control of his own movements any more and the fear of departure appeared to be collecting in hard, palpable knots. I would run my hand down his back and immediately feel them under his skin. Massage was the only thing that relaxed him. He would lie on his stomach and I would rub him down with baby oil. It gave him goose pimples because the oil was cold. Once my fingers started sliding down his neck and shoulders toward his spine and back muscles, a current of warmth would run through him, reddening his skin, and the knots would start to disappear, one by one. I would hear a soft groan, and then his even breathing as he fell asleep. I would keep massaging him. I do not really know whether I was merely massaging him or touching every smallest part of his body, every joint and vein, every tendon and curve, the better to remember it all. I knew this map by heart already, I knew all of its secrets. I would recognize his smooth stomach from a thousand others, his smell, the curve of his shoulders or thighs. Today I think that this was my way of saying goodbye to him, of making love to every inch of his skin. After a while, still half asleep, he would pull me down on top of him. I could hear his heartbeat quicken as he suddenly penetrated me, as if he could no longer stand so much touching, such closeness.

Never was he so close to me as in those last days, half asleep, yielding completely to my hands, to me. Later, when he was no more, whenever I went into the bedroom I would be startled by the sight of the empty, rumpled bed. The whiteness of the sheets without his strong, tanned body would take me aback. The fact that he was gone had not fully sunk in. I had not yet had time to get used to his absence, or to the way in which I would suddenly feel his presence. The sheets were soaked in his smell. His muscles had left such a strong imprint on the palms of my hands that at night, lying alone in that wasteland, I would feel as if he were still by my side. I wanted to touch him, to feel his living body. That magic touch, which would flood me with warmth. But all I could do was place my hand between my thighs and pretend it was his.

José's keenness to put his life in order and restore it to its previous state – the state it was in before he left for San Francisco, the state of unawareness of any pending separation – lasted barely a week. Suddenly, he collapsed, infected with his own weakness like it was the flu. My reaction was completely different. When I came back to New York I had a strong need to put an end to this superficial peace. I could not stand the uncertainty, this situation in which neither of us made a move, waiting for it to resolve itself.

It happened soon after our return to New York. We were sitting in a bar on Lexington Avenue late one evening. Going out was becoming increasingly tedious and tiring. We ourselves could see that we were moving apart. José started to hate New York. Love for the city which had enabled us to live together turned into open hostility, into a loathing which kept finding ever more justification: the wailing sirens of the fire trucks, the fire escapes outside the buildings, the garbage piled up in the streets at night, the stench of the subways, the whirring of the air-vents, even at the quietest of times, just before dawn. I began to taste in his kisses the city which was cropping up between us, pushing us away from each other. It rose up through his tongue, its spikes piercing my palate like the needles of skyscrapers. I could feel the membrane that held us together stretching too thin.

I knew that José would not last much longer.

That evening he mentioned death for the first time. We were sitting in yellow plastic-covered hard chairs, I remember. José was drinking vodka to get warm or forget, probably both. I was nibbling at the roasted peanuts in a dish on the table. 'It would be nice to die together,' he said that evening in between sips of his drink. 'To jump off the top of a skyscraper holding hands, so that nobody could ever again separate my body from yours, me from you.'

I broke out in a sweat at the pure vividness of the image. At the same time I was flushed with joy, as if José had just brought me some good news. Only now do I understand what it was that made me so happy that evening. It was the way in which he made a direct connection between our separation and death, his awareness that our love could end only in death. It was as if he was laying out the idea on the table for me. I saw the relief on his face, once he had said it. He had finally managed to articulate the nebulous, disturbing feeling he had been carrying around inside him for who knows how long.

I took his hand and pressed it against my face. José was trembling. His lower lip was quivering uncontrollably, as if it were a separate, mechanical part of his body. I knew that he was serious and that he was frightened of his own courage. It was as if he was sorry he had said it, I thought. But the words had been spoken, irrevocably. They lay on the table between us, like our blood had already spilled and was merging on the sidewalk. Had he stood up then, taken me by the hand and silently walked me down Lexington Avenue to one of the hotels between Fortieth and Fiftieth Streets, and had we then entered the hotel, taken a room, gone up in the elevator to the sixteenth or twentieth floor, opened one of the windows overlooking the street or the back alley, and, without looking down, tightly holding on to each other, had we stepped into the void . . .

I think there was a moment on that rainy December night when there was a serious possibility that we would have done it. A space for joint suicide opened inside us, like a sunlit field glowing at the end of a tunnel, as described by people who have experienced clinical death. But José slipped his hand out of mine and got up from the table. When he came back he was pale and beaded with sweat. 'I feel nauseous,' he said, wiping his forehead with a handkerchief. He was deathly silent the rest of the evening.

Seeing him hungrily drink in the moist night air as we hurried home, I reminded myself of what I had realized on the way to the airport in San Francisco, that I was the one who would have to bear the brunt of the decision, whatever it was. He walked two steps ahead of me. I followed him separately. This time we did not hold hands. I felt completely alone. I think we both realized that death had moved into the void created by those two steps.

José was running away from it. I was following it, the way a stranger in an unfamiliar landscape has to follow signposts.

That evening I think José and I came to some sort of an agreement. Not explicitly, because we certainly did not talk about it, but through small signals and movements. We were both aware that this agreement, however tacit, was more trustworthy and more secret that any written pact could be. It was an agreement about us and between us, and we knew that it was as real as food, drink or sleep. Perhaps that evening on Lexington Avenue we realized that neither of us could bear the thought of living without the other.

Still, there was time enough left for us to enjoy ourselves.

No more mention was made of joint suicide, but I noticed that José was worried about me. Though I was perfectly healthy, he began asking me how I felt and if I was all right – questions he had never asked before. Maybe he thought that I might kill myself, that one morning he would wake up to find me lying dead in the bathtub with my wrists cut. I was both moved and saddened by the thought that he worried about me like that. I did not have the strength to tell him that the idea had never even occurred to me, because it would mean excluding him, excluding myself from union with him. My suicide would have achieved precisely the opposite of the unity I was trying to maintain, that was so important to me.

'I could not go on living if something happened to you,' José told me one night as we lay so close to each other that the skin on our bodies felt as if it had melted away long ago, leaving my naked flesh stuck to his. Then he told me about a tribe of cannibals living in Papua New Guinea who were called Gini, whose women ate the corpses of their men. The Gini believed that this ritual gave men eternal life. 'Come, come to me, so that you do not rot in the earth. Let your body disappear inside mine,' says the Gini woman to the dead man as she eats his flesh, José told me. I felt that our bodies were already disappearing into each other and the Gini woman's tender call sounded perfectly sensible to me.

I now think that their kind of hunger finally became very familiar to me that night.

Several days later we were sitting in an Italian restaurant, cheerfully discussing renting a new apartment. We were talking over a plate of pasta with tomatoes, a bowl of salad and pieces of bread dipped in olive oil. It was as if nothing had happened in the interim, as if the future still lay ahead of us. It was a game, a rather painful game. José was reading the classifieds in the *Village Voice*. 'All we really need is one small room. That's enough,' he said.

'We can get jobs in some bar. You can be the barman and I can be a waitress,' I said.

My practical streak seemed to amuse him, because he laughed and said, 'But just one room isn't enough for life.'

It may, however, be enough for death, I wanted to say. But he had already gone to phone. I heard him inquiring about the monthly rent for the room. His voice sounded very serious. In the half-empty restaurant on a late winter afternoon his words bounced off the newspaper and fell into my plate with a piece of pâté. Slowly I spread them on a slice of bread and took a bite. The word 'couple' had a salty taste to it, and positively melted on my tongue.

So we rent a room overlooking Central Park, and then sit down in front of the window and eat pâté, just as if we were eating each other. We do not leave the room ever again. We eat each other, like the survivors in the Andes. First pieces of meat off the calves of the legs. Soon it would become unbearable. We would be bleeding from open wounds, watching each other die. One room was quite sufficient for that, I thought, as José returned to the table.

I thought how it would be better if he died first. Then I would live off his body all winter. I would not leave the room until the trees turned green again. I would go out into Central Park, pick a thin, green leaf and turn it to the sun. I would gaze at that green sun for a long time. Like the little leaf, I would be full of new life. 'Let your body disappear inside mine.' I would whisper the words of the Gini women as I walked through the park, overcome by the feeling of union.

*

Approximately two weeks before his death, José stopped all activities which might compel him to leave the apartment. He gave up going to the university and the library. He spent his time in bed. He slept late. Sometimes I would wake him up, amazed that anyone could sleep that long. In the intervening hours he drank and played chess against himself. The vodka and gin bottles piled up on the floor next to the bed. I would bring replacements from the store – he would not even go out for them. I would lie down next to him and he would draw me to him gently and rock me, singing softly in Portuguese. Those soft, sad-sounding words must have been a lullaby. Or else he would sit on the floor, put his arms around my knees and his head in my lap, and talk, talk, talk, in his own language, like a child confiding in his mother. I would cry. I did not understand what he was saying, but I knew that José was taking his leave of me. I would rest my head on his and weep.

And as we sat hugging each other, I saw his future life as plain as plain could be.

Summer in São Paulo. Workers are repairing Paulista Avenue and a huge cloud of fine, white dust spreads over the street, covering the shop windows like a fog. The sound of the drill breaks the day up into tiny, disjointed pieces. A truck screeches to a halt at the traffic light and José crosses the dug-up intersection. The crowd carries him away from the demolishing sound. He turns the corner, casting an eye at the news-stand. He rummages in his pocket for his car keys, unlocks and opens the door of his second-hand Honda. Getting into the car, he steps on a dog turd. He swears. The city is falling to pieces. Cities are nothing but piles of garbage. He drives behind a white convertible. At the wheel he remembers he has to hurry home today because his mother is coming to see them. Inês called at the university to tell him. He had jumped at the ring of the phone, for no reason. He had not been expecting another phone call. Suddenly, he sees something pink flash in his rearview mirror. It is nothing really, probably just a strange refraction of the light. But the pink colour is still there, and now he clearly recognizes the shade, the shade of her lipstick. The way she puts it on slowly, staring into his eyes. Later, with the palm of her hand she wipes it off his lips, neck, cheeks.

Suddenly, José feels the full weight of the city bearing down on him: the quivering air, the fine mist, the noise, the shafts of light refracted through the particles of dust, the scrap of paper stuck in the windscreen wiper. His sweaty hands turn the wheel sharply to the right and he pulls up at the kerb. He opens the door, walks into a bar and asks for a glass of cold water. The girl at the bar smiles politely. José sees that her lipstick is the same colour, and that makes him feel even queasier. He still does not know what is wrong with him, except that he feels saliva rising in his mouth, making him want to vomit. He gulps down the water. It makes him feel better. He does not look up, he cannot bear to see the girl's lips again. I have to hurry, he thinks, it's late.

He notices Felipe's ball in the car and is moved by it. On the seat next to him are crumpled paper tissues. Inês cried last night. They had gone to see a movie, and when they got back into the car she burst into heaving sobs. 'Why are you crying?' José had asked, lifting her chin. Yet another futile attempt to get close, he realized as his fingertips wallowed in her tears. She closed her eyes tight, as if she could not bear the thought of opening them and seeing him. He took a tissue and wiped her face. She cried even harder. Climbing the stairs up to his apartment overlooking the supermarket and the playground, he smells fish baking in the oven. He rummages in his pocket for his key. Suddenly he feels uncertain. He is standing in front of the door, caught between two realities. Every move seems to him unbearably difficult.

José was playing chess on a small electronic chessboard no bigger than a packet of cigarettes. I was lying next to him, watching him move the white pawn, which was so tiny he had to use his nails to pick it up. His nails were long, like a woman's. I was sure he had forgotten to cut them, just as he had almost forgotten how to brush his teeth and wash his hair. I had to tell him everything – get up, do that, do this – as if he were seriously ill or wounded. I would take him by the hand into the bathroom and soap him. The water and the touch of my hands would restore him. I could feel, again and again, that he was giving himself up to me completely. He was putting himself in my hands not temporarily, as happens when you relax your body naturally in the water, but permanently, as if he were handing ownership of himself over to me; as if he wanted to get rid of the burden of his own body, but could not do it by himself. He needed help. I cannot explain my feeling and conviction that this was so. I watched him sprawl out in the full bath, his body slowing rising to the surface. His face showed relief, even bliss, because of this incorporeality, because of the momentary possibility of disburdening himself of reality.

I had already forgotten about it, or maybe I had simply become used to the unusual way José picked up objects. He avoided touching them with his fingertips. At first I thought it was hard for him to pick up things that way, that he had to think every time he touched a doorknob, bread, shoes, whatever. But it was simply a habit. Still, I wondered what touch was like for José. Was it different for him? The fingertips are extremely sensitive parts of the body, as the blind know only too well. They say that some especially sensitive people can even recognize colours with their fingertips. When he first caressed me, José's hands were slightly stiff, his fingers awkwardly splayed. Fear of touching the unknown was how I interpreted it. When I noticed how long his nails were, I thought it was a sign of extreme neglect. 'Do you want me to cut your nails?' I asked.

José waved the question away as if I had asked it for the umpteenth time. 'Not now. Later maybe. I have to prepare myself for it first. When I cut them the skin on my fingertips becomes so sensitive that it takes me a few days to get used to touching again. Even when I was little I would hide my nails so that my mother wouldn't see how long they had grown. No, it doesn't hurt, but it does feel as if you have no skin there. It's as if the fingertips are flayed open. You feel as if the linen, wood or paper is directly entering you, creating an unbearable feeling of their presence.'

José spoke as if there was nothing odd about this.

I took a pair of scissors and picked up his hand. He did not pull it away. His fingers were long and bony. I clipped the nails, taking care not to touch the tips of his fingers. It was true: the ridges on the fingertips were barely visible and the skin was thin, as if depleted. Holding all his ten fingers in front of me, I realized that this was the most sensitive part of him; that this was where José connected directly with the world.

Slowly, carefully, as if wanting to make sure for myself, I licked each fingertip separately. He did not pull his hand back. Then I put his fingers in my mouth, letting his unprotected fingertips grope around, touch my palate, teeth, the root of my tongue and the wet membrane, just letting them be inside me, so that I could be inside him. His fingers turned into voracious polyps hungry for meat, penetrating my every opening, as if there were a thousand of them. It hurt, but I could not stop him; I did not want to stop him, because I knew that I was giving him my precious secret.

We should have died that evening. We would have died having satiated each other to the end. That was as far as we could go anyway.

IX

Once my mind had turned to death, it did not take long for me to make the decisive leap from two deaths to one, from our death to his, from the idea to its realization. It was as if José and I had actually started down this road that rainy night on Lexington Avenue. After that we both encountered the signs, but only I knew how to interpret them.

One day, when I was cleaning the room (God, it was less than a month ago), I found a French newspaper clipping under the desk. It must have slipped out of José's file. The clipping was already yellow with age and frayed along the folded lines. It was about Issei Sagawa, a Japanese man who, in 1981, in Paris, had killed his Dutch girlfriend, Renée. It was a famous case. Even in Poland we had read about it. Everybody who knew the couple claimed that they had got on well, and yet Sagawa had not only shot the girl dead, in the back of the head, he had chopped her into pieces, separated the flesh from the bone, put the meat in the refrigerator and used part of it to make *sukiyaki*. And that was after he had first eaten her lips, tongue and the tip of her nose. The rest of her remains he packed into two suitcases, which he intended to dispose of in the Bois de Boulogne. As it happened, he was identified by a taxi driver and arrested just two days after the murder.

I wondered how long it had taken, how long Renée had already been dead in his mind before he killed her. At his trial he said that this kind of hunger had been tormenting him for years, and that it was not just Renée to whom this had happened. It must have taken him time to plan everything. What happened in the meantime? Was it a matter of days, then just hours and then minutes? Did Renée suspect anything form his looks or words? And what was she thinking when he pressed the gun to the back of her head?

At the time the story had left me pretty cold, even though the press had touted it as an 'unprecedented case of modern cannibalism'. But reading the clipping that day, I saw it in a completely different light. When they arrested him, Sagawa said he had had to do it. He did not regret it at all. 'To me cannibalism isn't anything terrible, or dirty or criminal. Not at all. It's sort of an expression of love. I wanted to feel the existence of the person I love,' he said.

They did not believe him. They pronounced him insane and later released him. Another Japanese man wrote a book about Sagawa, based on his own correspondence with him. It sold three hundred thousand copies. Perhaps because Sagawa had described the taste of human meat, as if discussing the difference between chicken and pork; as if taste was the key, rather than the obsessive desire for total possession of another human being. Since he was declared insane, I doubt that anyone realized the importance of his justification. Sagawa explained his cannibalism as a kind of appropriation rite. But all everyone talked about was the brutality and bizarre nature of the act. No one took his explanation seriously. Reading and rereading the article, I suddenly completely understood his desire for total communion, his desire to interiorize the girl who so fascinated him.

I took the fact that I, not José, had found the article as an omen.

When I managed to stop and take a break from my manic cleaning, when I composed myself and tried to examine my own situation, I found it impossible to believe that so little time had elapsed between my final decision and its actual execution. What I remembered best was the moment when I finally found relief.

It was the day after I had read the Sagawa article. It was a Sunday and, as usual, I was making beef soup. I tried to make soup every Sunday, a habit inherited from my parents. Sunday lunches usually started with beef or chicken soup and then moved on to boiled meat and potatoes. On Saturday I had bought a good round of beef. On Sunday morning I took it out of the fridge, rinsed it and laid it out on the chopping board. It was a nice, long, two-kilo piece. I took the dark red healthy marbled meat, sliced it down the middle and put one half in the pot to cook with the carrots, parsley, celery and onion. I planned to put the other half back in the fridge, but instead I took my sharpest knife and cut off a thin slice the size of the palm of my hand. I divided it into six pieces and placed one in my mouth. The meat was quite tasteless and tough, but I chewed it anyway and swallowed it, piece by piece. This is how it must have been, I thought as I chewed the beef. Sagawa must have sat down in front of the wooden board in the kitchen of his Paris loft. He took a sharp knife and first cut off the tip of the nose, then the lips and then the tongue. I don't know why, but that seemed the most logical order to me. To eat it all, he first had to cut the meat into small cubes. There was quite a lot of blood, but that did not seem to stop him from immediately satisfying his hunger.

What was in his mind at that moment? What did he feel? And finally, really, what did Renée taste like?

He was sitting in the kitchen. Maybe it was a Sunday, too. He was listening to the distant ring of the church bells – morning mass had begun. Pigeons were sunning themselves on the drainpipe under the window which overlooked a patch of the square and a leafy tree. Issei Sagawa chewed each morsel slowly, savouring each piece. At last, he thought, at last I possess Renée completely.

I was sitting in the kitchen that Sunday morning dicing up the raw beef and eating it. Outside in the yard, a ginger kitten was playing with a scrap of paper and the boy from next door was parking his red bicycle. The head of a blonde woman appeared at the window across the way. I thought of the Japanese man and of José. When I had eaten the last piece of raw beef, I knew I had reached the end of the road.

I pressed my forehead against the cold windowpane. A wave of relief washed over me: the only true, the only possible answer was within reach. Suddenly, everything looked different: the kitchen became lighter, the objects in my hands weightless. Reality became arbitrary again, but this time the thought did not throw me into the depths of despair; instead it elated me.

Later, while we were eating the supper I'd prepared, I knew exactly what I had to do. I watched José eating his boiled beef, chewing rapidly, absentmindedly, a mouthful of meat, a mouthful of mashed potato, a mouthful of meat, a mouthful of mashed potato, and I wondered why he had not hit upon the idea himself. It was his subject, after all. He was the one writing a book about cannibalism, he was the one who had accidentally steered me toward this solution. Looking at it from today's perspective, I think the answer was simple. If it had ever occurred to him, José lacked the resolve to do it, and he knew it. Just as he knew that he would not have been one of the sixteen who had lived after the crash in the Andes, and that he certainly was no survivor. I think that toward the end even José was aware of all this.

It took me two or three days to get used to this new, now crystal-clear idea. At last I knew what I had to do.

I was now catapulted into a sphere where there were no more uncertainties or dilemmas. Now I saw everything from above. The fact that my love for José had a future made me feel as though I was standing on top of a tower or flying in the air, with a bird's-eye view of the landscape. People and objects suddenly became so tiny that I could barely make them out. And I myself, finally, without fear, had stepped into the future: I saw myself in the kitchen, opening the fridge inside which the pieces of meat were stored, neatly stacked and wrapped in clingfilm, like on a supermarket shelf. I imagined how I would get up every morning, put a piece of meat in my mouth, and, while chewing it, feel that José and I were together once more, that no one could ever separate us again.

José now went completely out of focus. I lived with him, but unlike him, I was already in another dimension. 'What are we going to do?' he would ask when he was not in a stupor.

'Don't worry, we'll think of something. I'll find a way for us to stay together,' I would say, running my fingers through his hair and kissing his forehead as if he was sick.

My words put him at ease. Yes, José was deathly ill. And when someone is terribly poorly, and you see that he is suffering unbearably, then it is only natural to wish for him to die. And you pray for the end to come quickly so that his suffering soul might find peace.

I had felt that kind of peace when I pressed my lips against my mother's brow for one last kiss. It had been early afternoon, hospital visiting hours. I knew it would be soon: the doctors had told us that we could expect her to die any day. I saw how death was taking up more and more space in her hospital bed. It emanated from my mother's skin, her hair, her eyes, the smell of her sweat and her soft sighs. Every day after visiting her in the hospital, I went to church to pray for her speedy death. I brought her flowers – narcissi, freesias, violets – whatever I could find. Walking toward her room that Monday evening, I sensed a change, an unnatural silence in the hospital corridor. I entered the room. The nurse was about to pull the sheet up over her head. My mother's eyes were already closed, and for the first time I saw how thin her eyelids were, blue at the corners. Her face was pale and serene, and that serenity spilled over on to me. All the heaviness which had been building up inside me over the years, ever since the onset of her illness, now disappeared. I rearranged her hair and pulled the sheet over her face myself. I lay the narcissi I had brought on her breast. I opened wide the window of her hospital room. The greenery came bursting in from outside, the top of the linden tree almost reaching through the window. When I pressed my lips to her brow, she was still warm.

So I finally knew what I would do about José. But I did not know how.

I had to start somewhere. Near the apartment I had

noticed a hardware store. I gazed at the shop window for a while, not knowing exactly what I was looking for. Finally I went in and immediately found myself standing in front of the knife rack. My eye was caught by a set of six large knives in a box which said 'all-purpose'. A grey box of six neatly arranged knives was something I could accept. But next to it was a real butcher's knife with a wooden handle. It looked so dangerous that it gave me the creeps. I could not imagine myself bending over José with a gleaming Swedish steel knife in my hand. I stood among the shelves containing kitchen equipment – juice-squeezers, blenders and coffee mills – looking helplessly at that sinister knife.

I went back, convinced that I could not do it – I could not take the knife and cut into the body of a person I loved, feel the blade entering him, encountering no resistance; find myself suddenly looking at the dark, still live red meat curling open like a flower; take a chunk of it in my hand, put it on the chopping board and slice it into small pieces.

I will not be able to do it, I said to myself walking home, as if the sight of the butcher's knife had physically debilitated me. As I was passing Kurowycky & Son's, on First Avenue, the butcher was hanging up half a pig. On the round wooden table behind him I saw the same sort of knives. Perhaps he had bought them at that same store. Kurowycky's was one of those old-fashioned butchers' shops, the kind that the Poles have. It had white tiles, just like at home, and the meat was not processed and prepacked. The young man (Kurowycky Junior, presumably) would cut off a piece from the large leg or shoulder of beef right there in front of you.

The half-pig the butcher had just strung up was clean

and pink on the inside. A thin, transparent skin covered the ribs, and the spine had been sawn straight down the middle of the vertebrae. There was no blood, and that made it easier for me. A woman wearing no coat walked in. She must have lived next door. The butcher wiped his hands on his apron and grabbed two knives off the counter. He spent a few minutes sharpening the blades against each other. I could see his strong forearms and hear the shrill sound of the knives, like a shriek. Then he grabbed the other half of the pig, which was hanging overhead. It was as if I had heard and seen all this before. Just before the gleaming blade of his knife plunged into the pink meat, I heard squealing.

I was five years old. We had been invited to a pig-slaughtering in Pawlowice. I was standing at the kitchen window overlooking the courtyard. The window was fogged over. I wiped clear a spot with my hand. Pavel, Jadwiga's husband, was chasing a pig in the muddy courtyard. A fire was burning in the corner and above it hung a big cauldron. Two women watched from the sidelines. They were wearing kerchiefs and white aprons. They were laughing. The pig managed to go around several times before Pavel caught it and threw it on to its side. He knelt next to it and in his raised hand I saw a knife. Then I heard a scream, a very human scream which pierced the doors and windows. The pig screamed once more, but the sound was fainter this time, more like a moan. Its hind legs twitched senselessly in the air, as if still running. Later, they strung the pig up by its hind legs and I saw that same knife sliding down its stomach, slicing it open. In the ensuing silence I heard nothing but the beating of my own heart. I was alone in the house. I stood at the window and cried.

When I opened my eyes, I was in front of the butcher's

shop, but the woman had gone and the butcher was reading the newspaper. I threw one more glance at the half-pig, as if that would release me from the scream that had been sleeping inside me all those years. However, I could not help noticing once again what a clean spinal cut had been made on the piece hanging in the window. And then I realized that a saw must have been used. Only an electric saw could have made such a cut.

I realized that the knife could be avoided.

It did not all go smoothly. There were moments when I almost gave up. Somehow I got over the first crisis, the one at the butcher's. The next day I went back to the hardware store. Now I knew exactly what I was looking for. But the saws on display were too big and cumbersome, I would barely be able to hold them, let alone handle them. On the wall was a poster of a man stripped to the waist, sawing through a tree with just one hand. The sight of his muscular body was enough to dishearten me and had it not been for the young salesman who came to my assistance, I don't know if I would have managed to buy the right thing. I would probably have bought the wrong saw and been unable to do anything with it when I got it home. How easy it would have been to give up. I was all nerves at the time anyway, constantly on the verge of hysterics. I felt I would never get past even the most basic of obstacles, like buying the proper tool for such an operation. I did not realize that once a person decides on such an act, there are still psychological hurdles to be overcome, and that has to be done gradually, like climbing stairs. These obstacles appeared to me in the form of mental images, like the one of the pig-slaughter. That was just the beginning. Then came the next phases, from the inability to make up my mind to the trembling hands, crying fits and insomnia. Resolve was not in itself enough. I think it was only then that I came to understand surgeons. They think about how they have to operate on the heart or the stomach and do not look at the person's face. A green cloth covers both the face and the body. An operation, that is what it will be, an operation, I kept reassuring myself, as if the word would protect me. I could already see myself in the sterile theatre. José's body was in front of me. The green cloth covering his face allowed no emotions to break through.

I could not let myself be daunted by these psychological reactions which, after all, were only to be expected. I had to find the strength to overcome them. I had to think of José's death as a task and contemplate the technical details. Once I managed to do that, the rest would follow naturally.

I do not know exactly when the psychological turning point occurred, perhaps not until I stepped into the hardware store. When the salesman asked me if he could be of any assistance, I already knew what I needed and formulated my request accordingly. I said that I needed a saw for wood. I wanted to make bookshelves, I explained. The young man reached behind him and picked up a small Bosch electric saw, with six different attachments for wood, metal, stone, etc. 'For house and garden,' said the brochure. I took it in my hands. It was not exactly light, but it was easy to handle. It looked just the way it should, like a precision surgical instrument. I walked out of the store whistling, as if I had just been given a nice toy for a present.

When I first saw the kitchen of the New York apartment, the first thing I noticed was the refrigerator. It looked so big. It was big, of course, but only in comparison with the one we had at home in Warsaw. And as it turned out, it was certainly not big enough to hold an entire man, as I had thought. The image of a refrigerator full of neatly stacked pieces of meat wrapped in clingfilm again crossed my mind. I was quite naïve and, I think, completely impractical. It never dawned on me that this huge refrigerator could be too small. It would not have been of any great help had I realized earlier, but at least I would not have found myself in the situation of having immediately to dispose of the pieces that would not fit into it. Even Sagawa had had that problem, and he had had to divide Renée's remains into two suitcases. I was pretty angry when I discovered that I would have to immediately throw away the remains of the body, because it was something I had not counted on. Furious, I slammed the refrigerator door, then the apartment door, then the downstairs front door. I stood in the street with a heavy bag, carrying a load I had to get rid of. I was sure that, unrefrigerated, it would soon start to smell. That was all I was afraid of, that stench of decomposition which clings to the walls, sheets, clothes and skin. My sensitivity to smells was unusually acute.

The first package of remains was the hardest. I stuffed it into a sports bag and took a bus. Somewhere around Fortieth Street an elderly lady, wearing sandals and no stockings, got on. I saw that her toenails were curved down like the beak of a bird pecking crumbs off the ground. She stood across from me, withered and bowed with age, wearing a thin dress as if winter was not upon us, as if it was not late December. She held on to the strap with both hands and started to sing in a reedy, almost childlike voice. It was a Christmas carol. The voice hurt me, like a scratch. I hugged my sports bag and rested my head on it.

There was no one left in this city, no one at all, to whom the timbre of my voice or my name might mean something. This unexpected thought kept coming back to me in the waves of her voice, and it made me cry. Later, when I emptied the bag's contents into a dumpster outside the Pig Heaven Chinese restaurant, where José and I had once eaten and laughed at the drawings of smiling pigs above the front door, I realized I was still crying. I went into the restaurant and found the toilet. Leaning against the wall, I listened to someone steadily peeing and that helped stop my fit of vulnerability.

A young Chinese girl came out of one of the toilets. She looked coquettishly into the mirror, but there she found my pale, rigid face. She turned to me and held out her compact. Powdering my face completely restored my self-confidence. I thanked her and walked out. The sky had just been given a fresh light blue coat of paint.

I decided that I was being overly sentimental and that I had to stop feeling sorry for myself and for José. The second trip was much easier. That same evening I took a taxi to Penn Station with another sports bag, which made me look like an ordinary traveller. I bought a return ticket for the local train to Newark. I planned to leave the package in a dumpster there and come straight back. But the carriage was empty, so when we crossed the bridge, I opened the window and tossed the bag into the water. It seemed simpler. Water or dumpster, it made no difference. I did not like thinking about it, it was a snap decision. I was terribly tired. My bag would sink down into the water or into the endless sea of garbage somewhere at the end of town, if such a thing exists here. When I closed the window, the matter was of no concern to me any more, at least not for the next few hours. I read a copy of *Newsday* that somebody had left behind on the seat and ate a packet of mints. At the station I waited for the train going in the opposite direction and dozed all the way back to New York.

Yesterday, after disposing of the last package, I treated myself to an ice cream in the West Village. I ordered a vanilla cone sprinkled with grated chocolate and real ground hazelnuts. It was late in the afternoon but the sun was still clinging to the building tops. I thought how none of this would have been possible in Poland. Not this kind of ice cream, not this kind of saw, not all this garbage New Yorkers started putting out in the streets at this time of day.

I began to change my opinion of New York garbage, which had bothered me tremendously at first, only after I made the effort to inspect it more closely. The big black bags which spilled out into the streets at night like punctured stomachs, the overflowing metal dumpsters in the back alleys, the blue cans on the street corners where dog-owners tossed their pets' turds carefully collected in plastic bags – all this aroused a deep sense of gratitude in me now. It did not disgust me any more. The huge amounts of trash had turned into one of the advantages of New York, I thought as the chocolate melted on my tongue. Looking down the street at the black bags which, in the encroaching darkness, melted into the building fronts, was like watching a huge graveyard.

For me, New York's detritus was exactly that. Depositing José's remains around the city dumps was a grave digger's job, but it had to be done. It was the only way. I could not simply fly off and leave the corpse behind. That would have been stupid. Of course, I could have tried to dissolve the remains in the tub with the help of hydrochloric acid, which I'd read about somewhere, but that seemed too messy and dangerous. I found the idea particularly off-putting because it would have made it look as if I had wanted to get rid of the evidence at all costs. That was not the point at all. If I had been able to stay in New York, I would have stayed with José forever. I would have bought a bigger refrigerator, big enough to hold his remains, and slowly I would have eaten them, exactly as I had imagined. Or else, had it been feasible, I would have taken him to Warsaw with me. The whole point was to consume his remains, not to deprive myself of them. Since I realized that I could not keep José's remains with me, the best thing would have been to cremate them. That way at least I would always have the urn with his ashes by my side. But I had to be practical. Of course it was impossible to have the dismembered body cremated. So there was nothing I could do except what I had done – to dispose of the remains in the simplest way.

The first thing I thought of, of course, was the garbage. Initially it struck me as humiliating and disgusting, but I had no choice. Ever since childhood I had been afraid of touching rubbish, of the stench of rot, of disease. I remembered how my mother would pass through the room and run her finger along the picture frame, a chair back or the books. 'Jadwiga, do you want to kill us? Do you want us all to die of disease?' Once when I did not want to wash my hands, Mother showed me an enlarged photograph of a maggot which lives in the dust. I looked at my hands, and then at the monsters with their beaked excrescences instead of a mouth, bulging eyes and web-like blobs on their armour. I could not imagine anything living in the dust, least of all these animals. I licked my finger to turn the magazine page. 'Now the maggots have entered your mouth,' she said. Suddenly, I had an image of monsters going into my mouth and attacking me from inside. I ran to the bathroom. Sobbing, I scrubbed my hands clean with a brush. It was only after she had cleaned them with alcohol, 'which kills those animals for sure', that I calmed down. I remember her gloves in leather, yarn, cotton and wool. She had a drawer full of gloves, for every occasion when she had to come into contact with reality. She was especially wary of doorknobs and hand rests on buses, and when I was little the disgusted expression on her face made me laugh. Later, when I grew up, I thought it was an affectation, a way of drawing attention to herself. But I never really discovered whether it was a genuine phobia or whether it concealed some other, more serious fear. She should have seen the people here who sleep among the garbage, and who get their food from it. She should have stuck her hands into a dumpster just once, or at least come near one. That would immediately have cured her pathological fear of maggots. My mother would never know how colourful and bright American garbage was, how different it was from ours. In American rubbish you could find whole loaves of bread, fine rolls, untouched cakes, barely nibbled apples or bananas, plastic dishes or ready-made Chinese food, big slices of pizza, oranges. And that was just the food. Then there were shoes, sneakers, socks, blankets, sweaters. I saw it all with my own eyes. Torn and dirty, but still wearable. The homeless lived off all this. Abandoned children and abandoned dogs, too. New York garbage was above all a feeding place, a dry, healthy scab on the organism of the city, and only secondarily a graveyard.

It would have been better to have had a place which I could mark properly with a cross, like a real grave, but that was not really the most important thing. As it was, the whole of New York would become José's tombstone. Every time I see a picture of New York or come back here, it will be like visiting his grave.

X

Just when all my plans were set, something almost went wrong.

Ever since we had come back from San Francisco, and especially in the last two weeks, we hardly went out at all. After his frenzy of work, José spent most of his time drunk in bed, as I've said, and I often climbed in next to him. We would lie there in each other's arms, clutching each other as if we expected an earthquake. An earthquake we could not escape. I think José would have been happiest if there had actually been one, or if a supernatural force had swooped in and crushed us. 'Do you hear? Do you hear? It's an earthquake coming,' he would whisper, but without fear. I sensed relief in his voice, but I think it was the vodka in him talking. He was not thinking about death. I know for sure that he wished for it. Maybe he felt it coming closer. But he did not have the strength to think about it. One thing was certain: he was not afraid of death. And so, consciously or not, he made my decision that much easier.

That Friday evening, Donna, the head of the Portuguese department, threw a farewell party for José. We did not feel like leaving the house, especially not for such an occasion. We did not talk about going home, but in front of others we had to behave more or less normally. We lived in anticipation of a solution but hid it from each other as best we knew how. He through drink, I by silence and planning. Of course, the dinner would be inconceivable without José. There were only six people and that seemed tolerable, a situation one could control. I knew he would quickly get drunk and then questions about his future in Brazil would not hurt him so much.

José was sitting between Donna and a woman photographer who had just returned from South America. They both spoke to him in Portuguese, but unlike in similar situations at the beginning of our relationship, this did not pose a danger to me any more. In fact, that evening I felt so self-confident that I was completely relaxed. José looked without interest at the food, the bowls of risotto and scampi, Greek salad, real *feijoada* (as our hostess so proudly pointed out), cold roast beef and corn bread. From what I understood, the two women were asking him about his book. He was drinking cold white wine and I could see from his face that he was trying to be polite and answer them. I could tell how hard it was for him to concentrate and to talk, not only about his book, but about anything. He was already far removed from everything.

Donna must have mentioned the case because of José's book. She probably thought he would find it interesting. The crime had taken place not far from her house, near Tompkins Square, where the homeless usually gather. Living in a nearby building overlooking the square was a ballerina. She passed by the square every day and would stop to talk to the homeless. She already knew some of them. Sometimes she would bring them food. It seems that one of them, a young man who called himself a poet, fell in love with her. He started to recite his poems to her. He was there waiting when she left her building, and again when she came back from town. At first she just smiled. His behaviour amused her and she did not pay much attention to him. Finally she could no longer avoid him. Every day he would block her path. Nobody knows exactly how he came to move in with her, whether she had eventually fallen in love with him too or whether she just felt sorry for him. Maybe she was feeling lonely that night and invited him up to her place. Anyway, for whatever reason, the homeless young man moved in with the ballerina.

For a while the ballerina continued to be seen. Spring came and the tepid sun and southerly wind slowly melted the ice. Accustomed to her hurried step, the inhabitants of the park soon noticed her absence. Some time between the last days of winter and the first days of spring, the ballerina had disappeared. Who knows what the homeless in the square thought? Probably that she had moved to a better, safer neighbourhood. But the poet still came by. He would bring them soup, occasionally with pieces of meat floating in it.

'Don't tell us any more,' said Donna's husband.

We were just about to embark on the Greek salad and his words caught Donna with her fork in mid-air. 'But José is an expert on cannibalism. I just wanted to hear his opinion,' she said. 'Anyway, the newspapers were full of the story and all its gory details.' He shrugged his shoulders. 'And so,' resumed Donna, 'it appears that the police did not believe the girl had moved away and disappeared without a trace. One day they entered her apartment and the first thing they saw was blood. There was blood everywhere: on the floor, the walls, the windows, even on the ceiling. They thought the stench would kill them. One of the policemen even fainted. Pieces of the girl's body were strewn all over the apartment. They found the poet in the kitchen. He was cooking the head. It was obvious that the man had eaten her flesh. That is how the police described what they saw.'

I still do not understand even today how she could have told that story at the dinner table. I had some salad left on my plate, mostly tomatoes. I pushed the plate away so abruptly that it clattered and I rose from the table. I went into the bathroom and sat on the toilet lid. The picture of the apartment where it happened was so vivid that it frightened me. I could see the black, dried blood on the mattress, the floor, the table. The trail led into the kitchen. On the kitchen door there was a clear set of handprints in blood. I could see pieces of the corpse lying all over the place. The young man probably slept like that, not even trying to clean up. When the police broke into the apartment, he had been cooking the head. Perhaps he never even heard them break in. And even if he had, he still would have stood there, stirring the pot with the girl's long, dark hair floating inside.

I did not switch on the bathroom light. I sat there in the dark, leaning against the cold wall. I could feel the growing pressure in my head, an iron vice tightening from the forehead across the temple to the back of my head, until it blurred my vision. I do not exactly know what happened. I presume I fainted and collapsed. I must have banged my forehead against the edge of the sink as I fell. When I opened my eyes, I was lying on the living-room couch and José was wiping the blood off my face with a wet cloth. He had found me lying on the bathroom floor. The cut was not deep, but it bled profusely. My tee-shirt was soaked with blood and when I raised my hand to touch my forehead, I saw that the inside of my hand was dark red. I started to cry.

I lay there in the middle of the elegant room, looking at the spotless white ceiling, and sobbed. Everyone probably thought I was over-sensitive, which in a way I was. But they could not have known, even José did not know, that I identified with Donna's story. When I mentioned the blood, José probably thought I was talking about the blood on my hands and clothes. He pulled off my T-shirt and washed my hands. But I was not talking about my own blood, I was thinking of the blood in the ballerina's apartment. Of the dried blood I had seen on the walls, and of my own fear of as yet unspilled blood.

I hesitated when I saw the blood on my own hands. The fact that it was my blood did not matter. The idea that I would get blood on me, that I could not avoid it, made me almost hysterical. If that happens, I thought, I will drop the dead body, run out into the street and throw my arms around the first man I see. Or I will do something completely impulsive. Either way it will ruin my plan. I was conscious of the need for control and of the fear of losing it, like two magnetic forces pulling me in opposite directions. Blood can be avoided, said my calmer, rational side. I cannot do it, my other side wailed.

I still remember that black-and-white photograph with the glue stains on the back. I always flip past that page of the album with its picture of my first communion. It shows a little blonde girl in a white dress, with white gloves, and a wreath of flowers on her head. The dress is buttoned up the front with twelve buttons covered in the same material, with another six on each sleeve. The little girl is holding her hands as if in prayer. She is wearing white knee socks and white shoes.

The preparations had taken months. First my father had brought back from one of his trips a swathe of white silk with a tiny floral pattern. 'Real Chinese silk,' said the seamstress knowingly when we went to arrange for the dress to be made. As she took my measurements, she talked about her brother in America who sometimes sent her good second-hand clothes. 'The fabric is so different from what we can buy here,' she said. 'Real camel hair, real tweed, real raw Shantung silk, real plain silk like this. You are a lucky little girl,' she said, pinching my cheek, as if I were getting married and had the great good fortune of a wedding gown made out of real silk. The fittings, the pins she used to hold up the sleeves, the cold touch of the scissors as she cut the opening for the neck, the whir of the sewing machine while I waited in my underpants for her to finish something off – all this made my first communion an exciting event. Then the visit to the cobbler, whose workshop was in the pantry. The whole floor smelled of leather and glue. His hands were black from the glue and as he talked, his little crooked knife would be cutting its way along the white patent leather. Mama ordered white lace gloves from the milliner. I think she did all the buttons too. She had several wreaths in her shop window, but for me she made a special one, adorned with shiny satin flower buds.

I woke up early that morning. The smell of cakes filled the entire apartment. Jadwiga had been baking for two whole days because we would be having a celebration and another eight children and their parents would be coming. Mama curled my hair with her curlers. She only did that for my birthday or when my father was giving a concert in Warsaw and she and I sat in the front row so that everybody could see us. When my hair was done, I put on my starched cotton petticoat, and then my new dress. Mama put the wreath in my hair and then I presented myself to my father. I remember that he said I looked like a princess. But he often said that, from which I deduced that he so admired my appearance that he could find no other word to express it. I was pleased. That was how I would look in the photograph, I thought. Just like a princess, full of myself. Except for my face. My face looked as if I was about to burst into tears any second.

Before setting off to the church of Saint Stanislav Kostka, I went to the toilet. When I pulled down my underpants, I saw a bloodstain. The window in the toilet was tall and narrow and it was always dark in there. I switched on the light and put my hand between my legs. It came out full of blood. I felt the toilet walls closing in on me and the window shrinking until it became a faraway speck of light. I felt as if I was in a prison and would never get out of it. I was bleeding. Sitting on the toilet seat in my white silk dress, I was overcome with fear. I was helpless. I was guilty.

I broke out in a sweat. There was nothing I could do. I did not dare call Mama, because then I would have to explain where the blood was coming from. I would tell her that I had cut myself, but how could I have cut myself between my legs? She would ask me what I had been doing, and I would not dare admit to her that yesterday Boris and I had played doctors and nurses at his house. He took a piece of glass and put in first on my tummy and then between my legs. He said it was an X-ray, and it showed everything really clearly. I must have moved or something. The glass cut me, but not badly. Boris was terribly scared, and I even more so. I held my hand there until the bleeding stopped. I did not dare put my underpants back on for fear of getting them dirty. The nausea set in as I was washing my hands.

Now the wound had opened up again, perhaps because of the rough ribbing on my underpants. All I could do was put them back on and hope that the bleeding would stop.

But all the way to the church, and as I walked up to the altar, I could feel the wet stain between my legs and had images of a treacherous drop of blood trickling down my leg, on to my white sock, spreading further and further down, until everybody could see that there was something wrong with me. I appeared before the altar dirty. I do not remember the communion itself, just my discomfort and the whiteness of the stone floor, which at any minute might turn red with my blood.

When I finally raised my eyes, they looked upon the large crucifixion behind the altar. Dark red drops of blood glistened on Christ's body, his forehead, the palms of his hand, his thighs. It became clear to me that blood was the sign of death, and that the moment when I first equated blood with death would remain sealed inside me forever, like a capsule of fear.

XI

Increasingly, I reverted to the past. It was like being attacked by it. Forgotten images would suddenly flash through my mind, inundating me with memories, like lava, as if every step in executing the plan was connected to some scene from my childhood or a suppressed emotion. I was going back to the past without even knowing it; there was a bridge between the present and the distant past, a firm link which I sensed, but did not understand. Sometimes I felt that what was happening to me had been charted long ago. At other times it seemed everything I did was deliberately calculated to take me back to my child-hood, to the feeling of being in total unison with the world around me.

I have been worn out and edgy these past few days, and to fall asleep I have had to block out all my senses. When I was very little, the touch of the soft flannel sheet on my mouth would help me go to sleep. I would draw the edge of the sheet to my face, and then rub my bottom lip with it until it began to prickle. Only then would I fall asleep. That was my body's earliest memory – the feeling of my lip falling asleep, after which I would be filled with a sense of peace, bliss almost.

I had already packed all my things into two big suit-cases. I did not want to have to add anything at the last minute. I had bought my father a new smoking jacket. I had noticed that his old one was frayed around the sleeves and collar, but he would have worn it for years without paying it any heed. He had embraced me when we said goodbye as I was leaving, and I saw how worn the collar was. Instantaneously, my father seemed even older to me. I had also got a present for Barbara, an Epilady hair-remover. She would be thrilled by this latest innovation. I could already hear her telling the neighbours about this new technique for removing the hair from your legs. She believed that life could be improved, you just had to have enough machines and appliances. I had bought new paints for Piotr. For my colleagues at the university I had a huge box of cookies shaped like the Statue of Liberty; for the nurse who took my father's blood pressure, and for the neighbours, some nicely wrapped soaps. Soap always comes in handy.

It was pitch black and quiet outside late last night. Looking out of the window I saw scattered snow. Snow muffled all sound. I do not think any of the neighbours were at home, not even the old lady. God knows where they are celebrating Christmas. Perhaps they were simply asleep. That is exactly what I would like to do: lie down, go to sleep and wake up somewhere else. In Poland, in my room, on the old brass bed. Or not wake up at all. Funnily enough, after having done all this, I have started thinking about my own death. It must be the fatigue. Had I stopped, had I given myself time, who knows what would have happened? Perhaps I would have been unable to control myself. Perhaps loneliness would have thrown me into the depths of despair. I knew that was a danger, so I kept on working, avoiding thought and emotion.

How can I explain that feeling of coldness, that gradual cooling which gripped me toward the tail end of José's life?

I never stopped loving him. There was not one moment when I was not aware of my love for him. But that love had moved to another realm. In reality I felt myself moving away from him, from this man in my bed, in my apartment. The bed had become my bed in my mind, the apartment my apartment. José was increasingly turning into an object. If I were a doctor I would say he was turning into a patient. I thought this must be how a prison guard feels when watching someone on death row. Or the executioner or hatchet man (what an ugly word), the one who thinks about the procedure and technique, about whether everything will function properly when the time comes. And perhaps the executioner also thinks about pain, because it is important for death not to be painful. I think I now know the reason why I deliberately distanced myself from José. I was simply preparing for the grand finale, for the solution to our situation. All my concentration, all my thoughts were focused on the execution of my plan. I was so tense there was simply no time for any emotion.

For instance, I had to decide the time, the day and the hour when I would finally kill José. And I had to calculate the number of days I would need to get rid of the body, clean up the house and pack and still be able to leave for Warsaw on time. I knew I did not have long and that therefore I had to prepare everything in advance and concentrate exclusively on the implementation of the plan. Perhaps I was like my father in that way. He was never nervous before an important concert. He was perfectly calm, but distant, as if only his body was present. He would talk, eat and sleep, but even as a child I knew that he was somewhere else. So it was now with me. José was still alive, we were living together, but I was already being forced to think of him as if he was no more, in other words, more or less as an article, a thing, an object. I also wondered how long it took the blood to coagulate in a dead body. That was a logical concern, because I wanted at all costs to avoid any unnecessary blood being spilled in the apartment. Not just because the sight of blood made me sick, but also because I did not want to give myself any extra work when cleaning up. The only thing I left for the very end was what to do with the remains. I did not have the strength to think about that then.

Sometimes I felt that José was sure to notice my absence, that empty anticipation of something that lay between us like an icy shadow. But then I would realize that it did not matter any more. I mean, I cared less and less what he thought, if he thought at all, because he seemed to be spending most of his time in a kind of mental and physical stupor. That sensitive ear for another being, that effort to catch the slightest change in the tone of voice or expression of the face, was over as far as I was concerned. It was easier for me that way, and nothing José said or did could change my plan. Unless he disappeared, simply walked out of the apartment, never to return. But that was out of the question. He was completely in my power, and he knew it. I do not mean that I was not excited about all these preparations, but this excitement in the face of uncertainty was counteracted by the fear that something would go wrong. I could not allow myself to even contemplate the possibility that something might slip out of control. Every now

and then I would know I was excited because I could iden-
tify the excitement physically, as a fire in the solar plexus or
a warm twitch which suddenly made me aware of my own
body.

I could not say how long this situation lasted before I
realized that in my mind it had all already happened – the
murder, the dismembering, carrying the remains to the
garbage dumps of New York – although in reality nothing had actually happened yet. It was as if I had fallen
into a state of limbo between the moment of decision
and the moment of execution. Sometimes I would feel as
if José's fate depended on me and me alone, and the
idea made me slightly euphoric. But that was an illusion.
Events had an inexorability of their own. Fate did exist,
but it was not outside us. Fate, my fate, lay in my character, in certain unchangeable traits of my personality. The
same was true of José. Had decisiveness of willpower
been built into his character, I am sure his fate would
have been different. In the final analysis, I was really just
a kind of facilitator.

From that period of limbo between the decision and its
execution, when my life was reduced to waiting for the
right moment, I remember a dream José told me about.
He dreamed it on his last night. It was about his sister. José
did not have a sister, but that night he dreamed that he
did. He was in an Indian village in the jungle. Perhaps he
was an Indian himself. It was night time. The men were
seated in a circle while an unknown woman was dancing
what looked like a ritual dance. She was wearing a white
death mask. At one moment she came up so close to José
that he could smell the warmth of her body. He could
smell her perspiring skin and a strong female odour. She
danced in front of him, or perhaps for him alone, and

there was something frightening yet appealing in her appearance, in the contrast between the naked, glistening body so full of life and the death mask. He felt a strong erection coming on. He reached out to the dancer, but she quickly moved away. In the next scene the woman was lying on a big dish. As he approached her, José saw that she was not moving. She was dead. She was lying on the wooden dish because she had been roasted and was being served to eat. A bowl of oil stood to the side. José picked up a feather, dipped it in the oil and began to brush it over her skin. Before picking up a piece of meat in his fingers, he removed the mask from her face. He recognized the dead woman as his own sister.

The dream was terrible in its obviousness, and I knew he must be aware of that too. José was lying in bed on his back, his head cradled in his arms. I snuggled up next to him. In the grey light of morning his dream had upset me. I could feel myself turning pale and my hands sweating. An uneasiness gripped me. Why had he told me about that dream on this last morning? And had it even been a dream, or was it a story he had invented simply to let me know that he knew what was in store for him? Why had he mentioned that the woman had been roasted and that he had planned to eat her? How did cannibalism enter his dream? José, however, did not seem upset by it. What surprised him most about the dream, he said, was that he recognized the woman as his sister; he was absolutely certain she was his sister. I recognized death, he said thoughtfully.

I got out of bed and looked out of the window. It was late in the morning. The street was grey with fog and deserted. A black man was coming out of Odessa, a coffee shop across the way. The sounds of reggae slowly wafted up to the bedroom window from the ghetto blaster on his shoulder. I followed his green cap and plaid jacket to the end of the street, to the stand selling Christmas decorations. Sentimentality getting the better of me, I wondered whether it was possible that José would never again see this sleepy street with its border of undersized birch trees, never again hear the sounds of reggae. The thought came to me because he had mentioned death again. The word 'death' coming from José's mouth, so clearly enunciated, caught me by surprise, as if I had suddenly gasped in cold air or church bells had rung out in the middle of the night.

Then I dismissed these ideas as ridiculous. If I maintained that death, José's death, was merely a transition to another form of existence, then that did away with any sentimentality and all forms of self-torture. Even if he had told me about the dream deliberately, so much the better. It meant that everything really was clear to him. What is more, it meant that he tacitly accepted whatever was to come. When I turned to look at him again, José was lying in the same position, his eyes closed. He was lying so still that I thought that he had stopped breathing.

It's time, I thought.

I do not know why, but that was when I realized that he had only a few hours left to live; that José would die that same day, that very evening.

I leaned over and kissed him maternally on the forehead, but he didn't flinch. I remember thinking that José would sleep through the last day of his life, instead of taking one last walk through New York, having a cup of good coffee, or doing something, anything, other than lying in bed and sleeping. What does a person do when he knows or senses that it is the last day of his life? I wondered as I closed the door carefully, not wanting to wake him up. Write a farewell letter? Pray to God? Dine well? Listen to music? Again, I remembered the man condemned to death and again I felt sorry for José. I felt a tiny, perfidious twinge of sadness.

Today I am of the view that it was better that he slept. It made it easier for both of us.

José had told me about his dream late in the morning, four days before Christmas. That dream and my decision to act coincided quite by chance. There were practical considerations, of course. I could no longer postpone my return to Warsaw for two reasons. First, the new tenants were due to move into the apartment before the New Year, and secondly, I had promised my father that I would be back by Christmas at the latest. I knew he expected us to spend the holidays together. The last time I had spoken to him was after I had booked my flight back, when I had already worked out the details of my plan. It was a brief conversation. I did not really have much to say to him, and money was tight. But during that short exchange I noticed that his voice trembled with suppressed excitement.

I do not know whether José overheard my conversation with the girl at Lot, and if he did, whether he understood anything. Or my conversation with my father straight afterwards. If he guessed I was making preparations for my departure, he said nothing. Now I think I was rather hard on him, because I behaved as if he were not there, even though he was. Yes, I should have done some things differently, more adroitly, more sensitively.

I was surprised how cheerful I sounded as I spoke to the Lot representative in Polish. When I put down the receiver I was overwhelmed with joy, because something we had both been waiting for had finally begun to unfold. It was as if at last I was embarking on a voyage fraught with uncertainties, but nonetheless pleasantly exciting and, therefore, slightly intoxicating.

At last I knew exactly what I had to do, and the order I had to do it in.

Nothing special happened that morning, apart from José telling me about his dream. He stayed in bed. In the early afternoon we ate lunch, a potato salad and an omelette, simple to prepare. I had put quite a lot of pepper and red onions in the potato salad, just the way he liked it. I remember José saying that the lunch really agreed with him. In the past two weeks we had been eating nothing but fast food – hot dogs, hamburgers, frozen dinners, cans of concentrated soup, even some tinned food. We had completely given up on our usual ritual of cooking and eating. That fact alone should have sounded the alarm: two people who turn every meal into a ritual suddenly, imperceptibly, finding themselves eating nothing but junk food. By giving up on real food we were giving up on ourselves, as if we were signalling to each other that death was already in our midst, in the empty refrigerator, in the cold, tasteless food, in the plastic fibres we were chewing unenthusiastically, but most of all in our lack of willpower to do anything about it. I am afraid this happened when we had no strength left any more, when our thoughts were elsewhere. Despair does not go with a hearty appetite, and José was in despair. I had no appetite either, nor did I feel the need to cook. Food meant nothing to me without José. And so, when he said the potato salad was excellent, I was truly touched. As if those simple words had immediately restored some of our former enjoyment of food, of eating itself. I was sorry, of course, that I had not done something better than a stupid salad. I thought of a cutlet with green peppers or roast veal with potatoes, or at least pasta with pesto. I started thinking about the salads and cakes I could have served with it, if nothing else a modest crême caramel, which José adored. I could have devoted more attention to his last meal, really I could have done. I was probably still subconsciously denying the fact that this was to be his last meal. I did not want it to be his last meal. I did not want José to die. I wanted us to live together. I watched the appetite with which he ate his potato salad and thought precisely that. I did not want him to die, I wanted him to live. And even though I knew that he would continue to live in me and through me, and that, paradoxical as it was, his death was our only chance to stay together, I felt so weak at that moment that I would have been capable of forsaking the plan if only I could have thought of another way out. These thoughts so saddened me that when José went back to bed and opened another bottle of vodka, I took a good swig of it myself.

Finally, I could put if off no longer. I went into the kitchen, took a glass, put ten sleeping tablets in a bit of water and stirred it until the pills dissolved. Then I added some orange juice and a few ice cubes. I took the drink into the room and topped off the glass with vodka. José was wont to add orange juice when he got tired of the taste of plain vodka. I held out the glass to him. He took it and threw me a grateful look.

Everything seemed perfectly normal. It was already getting dark, and the lamp on the night table was on.

The refrigerator could be heard humming away in the kitchen. The street suddenly fell silent and then a loud engine roared by. I was thinking that my head ached and that the weather was probably about to change. I went over to the window and looked out absently at the lit windows across the way. I avoided watching José drink the poisoned liquid. I did not have the strength for it. God, I thought, what happens if he drinks only half? Will it be enough, or will he wake up in the middle of the night? I would have to call an ambulance if he did. Numb, I anxiously turned around. Without thinking twice, José drank down his glass in long gulps. When he finished, he put the glass down on the night table, right next to the lamp. I cast a wary eye at the bottom of the glass. I was afraid that the tablets might not have dissolved completely and that I would see a telltale trace. Not because José, noticing the residue, would have realized what I was up to and rushed into the toilet to throw up, though he still might have done. What I was afraid of was the obviousness, the brutality of such a death. I think he would have been hurt by the transparency of my plan. By his behaviour José was letting me know that he agreed to a light, imperceptible, invisible death. Had I been less cautious, had my intention been visible from the very start, something inside him might eventually have rebelled. He might have taken steps of his own. Perhaps poisoned me. Perhaps, perhaps . . .

I sat on the bed. He looked like a sick man who was suddenly recovering. The brightness in his eyes, the rosy cheeks, the whiff of optimism. He took my hand. 'I love you,' he said.

'I love you too,' I said, barely getting the words out of my dry, tight throat. A wave of pain rose from the bottom of my lungs and filled me completely. I cried. There was nothing to be done about it. My shoulders shook with my sobbing, the coil which had been keeping my body under control let go. José hugged me tightly, as if only he could protect me against so much pain.

I cried like a child racked with pain, a pain that could not yet be articulated, and so not be soothed by anyone. How strange that that was the moment I should have turned into a child isolated by pain.

A part of me knew that there were only about ten minutes left before José fell into a sleep from which he would never wake up. The other part could not stem the desperate, uncontrolled tide of emotion. I lay down next to him. I leaned my head on his shoulder. José switched off the night lamp, drew me to him and wiped away my tears. His hand was warm and his touch soothed me. That was our farewell.

The room fell into pitch darkness. Outside it was getting colder and a transparent crust of ice was forming on the edges of the window. José fell sound asleep. He was breathing deeply, his mouth slightly open, with one hand lying on top of the cover. I still had a few hours before I had to finish off the job. After all that crying I felt rested, refreshed, perfectly at peace, as if the tears had cleared away the last shadow of doubt. Anyway, there was no going back now. And again I felt that strange sense of vigour and enterprise, as if I had embarked on a voyage. I got up and dressed quickly.

I went off to church. I had not planned this: I simply felt the need to compose myself a little. An icy wind followed me and, although the church was not far away, by the time I got there I was frozen through. It was pleasant inside. I was protected from the wind, from the cold, from my own disquiet. The small flickering candles lit for who knows whose souls, the smell of melting wax, the silence and semi-darkness all took me back closer and closer to home. In the pew in front of me a woman was fervently praying for someone's health. The flowers on the altar were fresh – they must have been recently placed there, because the pink gladioli and white roses still glistened with droplets of water. Soon evening mass commenced and the voices responding to the prayer echoed at length under the vaults of the half-empty church. I could not hear the priest very well, but I had a good view of his grey head, the flash of light on his glasses and the hand turning the pages of the book. Behind him stood a large statue of Christ on the cross. He had the usual drawn face, sunken cheeks and thin limbs. Almost all the statues of Christ I know show his ribs and a sunken stomach, as if he had starved and this was the only way to portray his suffering. At the end of the sermon – based on a parable from the Gospel according to St John – I stood in line to accept the wafer.

I remembered how José had once told me that Catholics were cannibals because they ate the body of Christ and drank his blood, and considered this to be the most exalted act of their religion. Yes, I thought, José is right. We whites and Catholics are cannibals too; it's not just the savages in Johann Froschauer's print, the Indians of the *terra nova*. Ever since I was a child, whenever I taste the wafer on my tongue I really do imagine that it is Christ's body, and I see nothing strange in it. I let the bland wafer melt on my tongue and then I take particular pleasure in piously swallowing it. Why should this kind of cannibalism be any different from that of the South American Indians, when both are a matter of faith, not food? As for me, the wafer really does represent the body of Christ, which I eat in order to attain union with Him in spirit. To me this is a natural and reasonable act, as is the connection between eating and the spirit. That evening it was with an equal feeling of utter certainty that I received the wafer from the priest's hands. They had red freckles, like my father's. And, with eyes closed, as I waited for the dry morsel to melt in my mouth, I was convinced that I was right: the fundamentals of my religion coincided with my intentions. I felt profoundly grateful to my mother, who had taught me to believe. Perhaps for the first time I understood how religion simplifies human life – and death.

On the way home I noticed a short-haired brown dog following me. It followed me from the church all the way to the butcher's, warily stopping every so often. When I turned around and crouched down, the dog first took two steps back, then sniffed me and wagged its tail. It had no collar and did not seem to have a master. It nuzzled me happily, and I thought how nice it would be to bring him home and feed him. Looking at the dog, it seemed impossible that anything in our lives had changed: I would go home and make an intricate, fine meal for supper. Perhaps stuffed breast of veal with a vegetable cream soup. Or Wiener schnitzel, or perhaps a light white fish in a sauce of olive oil, salt, pepper, crushed garlic and chopped parsley. I remembered that it was time to start making the Christmas cakes, the sweet, yellow sponge cake with raisins and a brown shiny crust, brushed with egg white. José and I would eat it straight from the oven, while it was still hot and aromatic, until our stomachs ached.

A gaping hole of hunger had just opened up inside me. Loneliness and hunger. As the dog moved uncertainly away, I felt the pit spreading down into my stomach. This was not ordinary, healthy hunger, which could be bribed with a piece of bread and cheese or a portion of French fries. This was an attack of hunger, like an attack of fever. Afraid I would faint, I walked into a nearby pizzeria. Miraculously, ten minutes later I was served a crisp pizza baked in a charcoal oven, with plenty of tomatoes. It smelled of oregano. I devoted myself to the meal, but it did not quell my hunger; if anything, this feeling was growing. I felt that I could eat at least one more pizza, and that was probably the truth. From now on I shall have to eat for two, I thought, the way at school you think of the next day's assignment. I will have to learn not to be afraid of this feeling of double hunger.

I drank a glass of wine. The clock showed seven. It was time to head home.

The window was dark, which was a good sign. José was asleep. Nothing untoward had happened. The building seemed alive now, the lights were on in almost all the windows. On the staircase I heard a strong stream of water from a bathroom. That was the waitress having her shower before going out for the evening, I thought. I could hear Mack's loud steps on the third floor, which shook the wooden banister. Somebody was cooking cauliflower. There was the sound of the television, music. An evening like any other.

I walked into the apartment, switched on the hall light, took of my shoes and slipped off my coat. I was greeted by the smell of alcohol. It must have smelled like that before, but I had never noticed it until now and suddenly it bothered me. The room was stuffy. The night lamp was on and I saw that José was lying in the same position he'd been in when I left him. I leaned over him. His lips were dry and slightly cracked, his forehead beaded with sweat. I gently lifted open the lid of his right eye. Only the white showed. I picked up his hand and then let it drop on to the cover. It was as limp as a rag. José did not stir.

There was still the last step to be taken.

I grabbed my pillow and pressed it against his face. I held it down as hard as I could. I looked at the clock. The phosphorescent dial said it was seven fifteen. I decided to hold the pillow down like that for at least half an hour, just in case. For the first few seconds José did not move. I pressed harder; I was afraid air might be coming in from somewhere. I felt the short jerks of his leg. It was the reflex reaction of a drugged body, the last unconscious spasm of a drowning man. He twitched two or three times and then fell still, finally surrendering to death.

I looked at the clock again. It had taken only seven minutes. José had to be dead already. Still, I did not ease my pressure on the pillow immediately. I leaned on it with all my weight and waited. I lay my head on the pillow. I could smell his sweaty hair underneath me and I ran my fingers through it. Even in the light of the streetlamp you could see he was already turning grey. That touched my heart. Suddenly I was afraid I would start remembering the past. Not now, I said to myself, not now. Perhaps that is how I shall spend my time in Poland, I thought, remembering his smell and the first time I ran my fingers through his black hair in the bathroom of his student apartment. As I lay on top of him like that, Poland seemed closer than ever and much more real than my crumpled, almost forgotten plane ticket. Or than the language I did not speak, because it did not mean anything to José. Poland. All this time it had been just a messy heap of manuscript papers on my desk, a few books, voices at the other end of the phone. And words uttered in moments of passion, because I knew them in no other language. When we were together, Poland took me away from José, so I deliberately tried to forget it, the way one deliberately suppresses an unpleasant event from the past. Lying there on the pillow, José's still body underneath me, I realized for the first time that in three days I would be going back. I still could not say 'home' – I associated the word too much with my life here in this apartment with José, with his body, lifeless and limp though it was now.

The blaring television grew louder, the way ours used to when my father turned up the sound for the evening news. Suddenly the mouthwatering smell of fried potatoes wafted past me. My God, I thought, is it possible that in this land of potato chips someone is actually frying potatoes? The way my mother used to, maybe? My mother sliced the potatoes into thin rounds and fried them in hot oil to make them crispy. I would eat them with my fingers as she removed them from the pan, and the warmth of the kitchen, the smell of oil mixed with the scent of my flannel nightgown, lulled me into a feeling of perfect tranquillity. Then I would lie down in my cold bed, and soon it would pick up the warmth that spread from my stomach and I would fall asleep. Sometimes my mother would come in, take my hand and sing me a lullaby. *Luli, senny mój aniołku, luli dziecię moje, na twe czołko, o fiołku, spuszczam słodką łzę* . . . I hummed it half aloud, whether to myself or to José I do not know. I was sure that he finally understood me. Where he was now, he finally understood my language; he understood all languages. He knew that I was filled with a pleasant fatigue and that it was all over.

At last I rose from the bed and removed the pillow from his face. I touched his forehead, like a sick man's. His skin his face. I touched his forehead, like a sick man's. His skin was sticky with sweat. I gently kissed his closed eyes. There was no frown on his fine, pale face. He looked as though he was sleeping peacefully. I heaved a sigh of relief. It had been easier than I thought. I lifted the sheet to check for a heartbeat. There was none.

XII

I had given my next move a lot of thought. José was dead because that was the only way for us to stay together. But death itself was not enough. Something else had to be done, something that would definitively unite us. There was only one way that José could continue to live inside me. Of course, I had thought about getting pregnant – that was the first thing that would have occurred to any woman in my position. But that would not create the kind of perfect, total unity, the union of body and spirit, that I was seeking. A child, even if it was his, would be an utterly new, separate being. I could never look at the child and say that he was José, no matter how much he might resemble him.

I thought often of the section in the book *Alive* in which Canessa eats pieces of human flesh for the first time. For him, and for all the sixteen survivors, eating the flesh of their dead comrades was an act of communion, and as they said later, they would never have been able to do such a thing had their faith in God not been strong enough. And truly, I thought, is there any more simple and more lofty act of union with the spirit than taking the wafer?

'Eat of my body . . .' Christ had said.

And I said to myself: 'I shall eat of his body so that José

may continue to live inside me. We shall be one. In spirit and in body. Amen.'

My decision was simple and pure and since it was based on love and faith, no moral doubts plagued me. But the decision was one thing, and reality quite another. The romantic idea of living off José's body for months until he pervaded my every cell, was, of course, out of the question. For reasons of time, I had to be practical. I knew that I would have to decide which parts of the body I simply could not give up. I had no option but to choose those parts that would symbolically represent the whole, and that was something I had not thought of in advance. I remembered Sagawa, and then the homeless man in Tompkins Square. When I thought of the mess they left behind them, I felt faint. I hate dirt and disorder, and the idea of living with the remains of a dismembered corpse for days on end truly horrified me. But they had been men, and probably did not notice disorder around them. I imagined it more as an elegant surgical operation which would leave no messy traces, no traces at all, in fact. That is why I intended to perform the main operation in the bathroom.

As I was lying on top of the pillow, my eye was caught by the sight of José's hand stretched out on the bed. He had long, fine fingers with nicely shaped nails. He had a firm, sure handshake, although he was careful to keep his fingertips free. That made his handshake somewhat unusual, because it seemed that he shook hands reluctantly, hesitatingly. It took some time for his fingertips to get used to my skin. Which is why in the beginning his touch was as light as the wind. Again I remembered his story about the sensitive cushions of his fingertips, and how as a child he had often suffered because of them. I imagined a little boy who shuddered at the touch of a rubber ball, a woollen scarf or a bark of wood. I imagined the difficulty with which he turned the pages of a book, unable to explain to anyone that the touch of reality was too rough, sometimes unbearable. 'There are no obstacles between you and me. When I touch you I feel you entering directly inside me,' he told me later, when my skin had tamed his fingertips. At first it was hard for me to imagine this heightened sensitivity he had. But now I was sure that his fingertips were indeed the most tender, the most sensitive part of José. By confiding his awkward secret to me, it was as if he had bequeathed them to me. I turned on the night lamp and drew his hand closer to the light. I did it without any difficulty because rigor mortis had not yet set in. His fingertips were prominent and pale, with a fine skin which had barely any of the characteristic patterns.

I went into the bathroom and picked up a towel, a razor blade and a packet of tissues. I knelt down next to the bed. First I placed the towel under José's hand, and then a tissue under each finger. Using my thumb and index finger I squeezed the tip of his little finger. The razor blade slid smoothly across the flesh and several large drops of blood fell on to the tissue. I was left holding an almost perfectly round piece of finger, thin and bloodless somehow. There was almost more skin to it than flesh, probably because I had been afraid to cut deeper.

José has been started now, that was my first thought, as if this act confirmed his death. I placed the round piece of meat on my tongue. I tasted the salty taste of blood. I held it on my tongue for a minute to appreciate the full sensation, as if I was waiting for it to melt. I was fully aware of the gravity of this moment, a moment in which I was breaking a taboo. But I swallowed the meat without difficulty. Indeed, it gave me a joyous thrill. Yes, at that moment I must have been intoxicated with a sense of my own power. I had wanted to possess José completely, and now I did.

I was a bit more careful with the other fingers. I held them so that the razor blade cut more deeply, almost down to the bone. Although I tried to avoid it, I got quite a lot of blood on me in the process, because his fingertip had bled profusely. I must have completely forgotten how blood would squirt from my own finger whenever I accidentally pricked myself on a sewing needle. I remember when I was having some tests done at the employment centre, a thin spurt of blood came spewing out of my middle finger. The nurse had laughed and said, 'Oh, it's nothing, you're as healthy as a horse,' even though the blood looked kind of pale to me. Once I cut myself on a broken vial of penicillin, and I still have the scar on my thumb to prove it. It was in the summer, and my white cotton blouse was soaked in blood. I was scared I would lose all my blood and I did not calm down until the doctor stitched it up.

But blood did not spurt from José's fingertips, it trickled, as though he were still alive. Each time I cut off a fingertip I would put it in my mouth, shut my eyes, wait for a moment, and then swallow it without chewing. I would be lying if I said I was not curious about the taste of human meat. Especially as they say that it has a special taste all of its own. That may be, but I did not notice it. To be honest, I have to say I did not notice any real difference between the cubes of raw beef and the cushions of José's fingertips, other than the taste of the blood. It was better this way, because I was afraid I might throw up as it was. I thought I might find it easier if I cooked or roasted the meat first. I was almost sorry that, with so many cookbooks around, there were no recipes for human meat.

Meanwhile, the house slowly settled into the quiet of a

winter's night. It must have been past nine o'clock already, but I was not paying attention to the hour. Not once did I hear the front door open or the usual wail of police sirens. Total silence reigned, as though, without knowing it, the neighbourhood was paying its respects to my little formal ritual.

Slicing off the tips of human fingers with a razor blade sounds relatively simple, but it was no such thing, as I discovered. First of all, I had to hold the blade in my right hand in a way in which I would not cut myself, pressing the middle down with my thumb to make it bend. But, it happened all the same, and I knew I had cut the tip of my own third finger. My blood was now dripping on to José's hand, and for a moment it looked as though the situation had been reversed, and it was he who was going to eat my meat. My lighter blood mixed with his darker, thicker blood, and when I ate the third slice of his fingertip I thought how I could just as easily have eaten my own. The taste would have been completely the same. My clumsiness reminded me of the children who play at being blood brothers, admittedly a game more popular among boys than with girls. First you take a piece of glass and draw blood from it from your forearm. Then each boy presses his wound against the other's to 'mix their blood'. Thus they become blood brothers, just like the Indians we used to read about, probably in the books of Karl May. It was a childish thought, because our two bodies had become 'blood brothers' in a far more perfect way.

Halfway through the job, just when I was about to move to the other hand, I had to take a break. I had to change the towel and throw away the dirty tissues. I noticed that my hands were shaking and that a dull ache was throbbing at the back of my neck. Perhaps I am coming down with the flu, I thought. I placed the clean towel underneath José's other hand and went back to work. But it was not the flu, it was something far more dangerous. I did not recognize the symptoms: the palpitations, pumped-up adrenaline, clammy hands, dry mouth and manic movements. At one point I did notice that the pieces I was cutting were getting bigger and bigger and more and more irregular, as if I were not paying proper attention to what I was doing. Only then did I realize that something inside me was making me voracious. The cushions of his fingertips were no longer satisfying my growing hunger.

I wanted to get as much of José inside me as I could.

Once I had swallowed all ten fingertips I could not stop there. The razor blade was too small to cut off larger chunks, so I went into the kitchen and fetched the sharpest knife I could find. First I sliced off the meaty cushions at the bottom of each thumb. Then I cut two long strips off the soft part of his forearm. I took the meat into the kitchen and chopped it up on the board, like beef for goulash. I was probably hoping I would be able to swallow it without chewing, but the pieces were too big and I was impatient, so in the end I had to chew José's rather tough meat. Even then I did not notice any particular taste. I think that was because an unpleasant feverishness had taken hold of me, and I could not concentrate on the taste. Maybe I was unable to taste it because of the vodka I had gulped down between mouthfuls.

I would not say that I enjoyed sitting there in the kitchen, eating the meat. It no longer had anything to do with ritual, or with the ceremonial pleasure I had felt initially. This was something I had not foreseen. It was as if I were in the grip of some drunken stupor or madness beyond my control. I was conscious of everything, but I behaved like a robot. I felt as though my body was being controlled by some mechanical power stronger than my own will.

Holding the sharp knife in one hand, I found myself at one stage bending over José's sleeping face. With my other hand I touched his lips, wondering what would be the best way to cut them. His lips attracted me now just as much as they had in life. I do not remember, but I must have thought I simply could not give them up. So there I was, leaning over his face, half conscious that my tormenting hunger for his body had nothing to do any more with the ritual of union in body and spirit, but rather was a wild desire to gorge myself on his meat. That must be what an animal feels like when hunting its prey, or how a man dying of starvation feels when he finally gets hold of some food. I was sufficiently composed to register that something extraordinary was happening to me, something I had not anticipated, and that this craving for raw human meat could lead me in the wrong direction. But how to desist? The hand with the knife was already quite close when something in José's face stopped me. His face was unshaven, and with the heavy blue bags under his eyes, it looked tired. Yet not even death could deform his clean-cut features. What had stopped me was his serene, extraordinary beauty, a harmony I did not have the strength to destroy. I sensed instinctively that it was something I had to respect. I leaned over and kissed him on the brow and then drank down some more vodka.

Suddenly I was overcome with fatigue. My hands were heavy and my fingers sticky with coagulated blood. I went into the bathroom. Rinsing the blood off my hands with warm water, I glanced at the mirror above the sink. My mouth was bloody like an open wound, or like the snout of a beast poking into a carcass. I stood there in the bathroom looking at that face, which just then had nothing in common with mine. I shuddered. A long, cold chill ran down my back. I felt beads of sweat trickling down my temples and sliding along my neck toward my breasts. I wiped my forearm across my forehead and lowered my eyes. No, that was not me. The eyes observing me had been the eyes of a person in the grip of an unknown passion. A person who, for a moment, had lost her mind.

I was afraid.

There, in front of the mirror, for the first time, I was afraid of what I had done.

I was not pleased to see the other side of my own personality, my inner side, my otherness, so terribly bloody. Again, I remembered Sagawa. Had this happened to him as well? Had he stood, blood-splattered, staring at his reflection in the mirror? But he had done what I had not dared to do, I thought, as if in self-defence. He had disfigured Renée. He had cut off her lips and tongue, even the tip of her nose. I had laughed when I read that. The tip of her nose! How did he ever think of that? Still, the very thought of it made me totally disgusted with the Japanese man. I was disgusted with myself for even thinking that I could have done the same thing.

I went back into the bedroom, switched off the light and lay down next to José. Before drifting off to sleep, I looked at the clock. It was seven minutes to midnight.

The glaring light woke me up. I opened my eyes and saw a pale sun shining outside, its light bouncing off the white walls of the room. When I closed them again, the room became pink. I liked waking up, that first moment when I opened my eyes and faced a new day. I amused myself with this game for a bit, stretching under the covers. When I finally got out of bed, I was disheartened. It was already after ten, and I had so much to do.

José was lying as still as before. I noticed that there were blue blotches on his chest, like some sort of stamps, and that turned my stomach slightly. When I touched his hand, it was cold and stiff. I withdrew my fingers as if I had burned them. I do not know what I expected exactly. His was the first corpse I had ever seen up close in my life.

I put the coffee on and things immediately looked up. As the espresso machine gurgled happily away, and the familiar aroma of strong black coffee filled the kitchen, I felt light, as if I were floating an inch above the ground. I even start to sing. Everything was fine, everything was going according to plan. I sat down to eat my breakfast. First I put quite a lot of whipped cream in my coffee, which was not my usual habit, and then I ate two pieces of bread with butter and apricot jam. But that only partly appeased my hunger, so I boiled an egg and had a bit of Italian salami that had been hanging around the refrigerator for days. I left the walnut rolls for the end. I felt strong and buoyant, although I was perplexed by these repeated attacks of hunger. I immediately associated them with fatigue, with nerves, with the change in weather and PMS. But I knew myself well enough to know that this insatiable hunger was something new. Perhaps this chronic hunger might continue, and I would stuff myself with huge quantities of food. I would eat more and more, and my stomach would get bigger and bigger. When they asked me if I was pregnant I would answer ambiguously: maybe. In the end, I would be so fat that I would barely be able to move. Strangely enough, the thought of my own grotesqueness did not scare me. It made me laugh. I must have believed at that moment that this was a phase of tension which would soon pass – something, I admit, of which I am growing less and less sure, considering the enormous amounts of food I have downed in the past four days. What else could I do except eat, eat, eat, in an effort to stave off the craving I felt last night, the craving for human meat? Fortunately, I had the fortitude to stop, otherwise I would have wound up like Sagawa and the poet. The new tenants would have discovered me sleeping in a blood-soaked bed with the disfigured remains of the corpse, which could no longer be called human. They probably would have locked me away in a lunatic asylum.

Maybe there is an ingredient in human meat that drives anyone who tastes it into temporary madness. Or perhaps you go mad because you have broken the greatest taboo, which relieves you of the responsibility of being human and therefore of abiding by human laws. I don't know.

While I was munching the walnut rolls and washing them down with coffee, another question crossed my mind: how was it possible that last night, when I was deciding which part of José's body to eat, I had never even thought of genitals? Because if we are talking about symbolically eating the parts rather than the whole, then that would have been the logical thing to do. But for me there was no sexual, no erotic connotation to the act of final union. Eating his flesh did not arouse me sexually. For me it was mainly a matter of satisfying my need to totally possess another being.

Mind you, there was still time to consider this. I went into the bedroom and lifted the covers. José's shrivelled penis looked like a little sleeping animal. It had withdrawn into itself, like a frightened snail. I knew that my fingers would never again feel it aroused, feel it grow; never again would I experience his ability to fill me to the hilt. That is probably the price I have to pay, I thought sadly, looking again at José's sleeping snail.

But was it still José? Or was it just corpse, a receptacle emptied of content? I still called him by his name, it was less than twenty-four hours since his death, but there was no sense in it any more. When I repeated José's name to myself, I thought of the living man, not of the corpse. I decided to put myself back in the role of a professional, neutral figure, like a pathologist. If a pathologist were to become intimate with his corpses, how would he ever do his job? Of course, the advantage the pathologist has is that, unlike me, he is not personally acquainted with his subjects. In order to achieve what I intended, I had to delete the person, erase the face and think only about the technical details of the procedure.

For instance, how to move the corpse from the bed into the bathroom.

I could not saw him into pieces on the bed. That was out of the question. Even with the greatest caution, I could not help staining the mattress, perhaps even damaging it, and that would be extremely ungrateful to the owner. I paid only four hundred dollars a month for the apartment and so I felt I should be even more careful. The wooden floor in the bedroom was no solution, either. But somehow I had to get him into the bathroom, that I had already decided. It was not far away, only five or six metres. But José was a tall, hefty man, alive I think he probably weighed ninety kilos, and dead and already rigid he certainly felt heavier. First I grabbed him under the arms, hoping to be able to pull him on to the floor and into the bathroom. But I couldn't even budge him. I wished I had read more detective stories and less poetry. Maybe then I would have known something more about handling corpses.

I forced myself to think practically: I lifted up one end of the sheet and pulled. The corpse rolled into the middle of the bed. That was the solution. I wrapped him up in the sheet and pulled the bottom edge where his feet were on to the floor. The dull thud of his head against the wooden floor made my flesh crawl. I was afraid his skull might have cracked and that I would have to spoon his brains off the floor. But the bed was low and probably the only thing that snapped were the cervical vertebrae, and they did not matter any more anyway. José was as heavy as if he had been made of stone. It took me quite a while, fifteen minutes maybe, to drag him those few metres and roll him into the bathtub.

When I had done that, I went, panting and sweating, into the kitchen to make myself another cup of coffee. I turned on the television in the living room. *Dallas* was showing on one of the channels. I could not follow the story and the dialogue all seemed funny and stupidly histrionic to me, but I needed a break. Sitting there in front of the television screen, I started thinking for some reason about watermelon. A big, green juicy watermelon. I had dropped one in the market once. The inside was red and wet, like human meat.

There was no point in putting off the most unpleasant part of the job any more. I knew that what was to come was a kind of funeral for José's remains. (I like the word remains; it suggests the idea that only the body is left behind and that the soul has found its resting place.) An unusual funeral, to be sure, but that was by force of circumstance.

In the kitchen I took the electric saw out of its box. It came with six different-sized blades: one for wood, one for iron, one for plastic, and so on. I picked the short one with small teeth 'for wood and artificial materials'. Mostly because it was no more than thirty centimetres long, and so seemed appropriate for use in the tub. It was simple to attach – you just turned a screw. When I plugged it in it, the saw began to hum pleasantly, and that gave me self-confidence. I took the saw and the chopping board and cheerfully went off to the bathroom, convinced that I would finish the job that day. I had to decide where to begin. Whether it was because my imagination had run dry, or because it was merely the simplest solution, I decided to start with the arms. First I spread a black plastic rubbish bag on the floor, on top of that I placed a big towel and on top of that newspapers. Although I had no experience or guidelines, I thought this would be the best way to absorb the blood. I lay the corpse out in the tub, mostly because I was afraid of all the blood that would appear once I cut into him. It was best to let the blood run into the tub: that way the apartment would not get too soiled. I knew that blood eventually had to clot, but I did not know how long that would take. I had no time to waste.

I put the board on the edge of the tub, underneath his right arm. I wanted to test the saw just below the elbow, because the bone of the forearm is not as thick as the thighbone or as wide as the breastbone. I turned on the power and knelt on the floor. I held the arm firmly down on the board with my left hand and pressed the saw against the skin with my right. The saw reached the bone in a second. Although it was what I feared most, there was no blood. That is to say the blood did not gush, it dripped, mostly from the pressure of my hand. At either end of the cut, the saw spewed up small particles of meat, like sawdust. I pressed harder. The sound of the saw changed, probably because the revolutions had slowed down. White bone shavings now appeared in the gash. It was not long, two or three minutes maybe, before I had sawn off the first piece. I put down the saw and stood up. I felt strange, a bit stupid, holding that piece of arm. I put it on the floor, threw a cursory look at the 'wound' – what else could I call it? – and noticed that the flesh was lighter in colour than I had expected. Still, I was glad that it was a straight, relatively clean cut, almost as if made by a professional.

This first cut was also important because I did not know how I would react, physically, I mean. The sawing could have made me so nauseous that I was unable to go on. I thought of the stories medical students tell about their anatomy classes, where fainting is very common. Not everyone has the stomach to dissect a corpse. Still, they told me that it is something you get used to. Few are so sensitive that they give up medicine because of it. I once knew a girl who was studying to be a vet. She could not make herself dissect a dog. Perhaps if the subject had been a pig, or even a cow, she would be a vet today. But it had been a beautiful Irish setter, and when the time came to slit open its stomach, the girl did not faint, she burst into tears. She never returned to the university. It is just as well that I remember her story, I thought, because it has brought me back to reality. This is not some anatomy test, I have not studied either medicine or veterinary science, and even more important, I had no choice. Nobody could do this in my stead. I kept mumbling these words to myself like the Lord's Prayer, aware that my tee-shirt was soaked with sweat. I stripped myself naked. That was simpler, since I had not thought of getting the proper gear – a big rubber apron, rubber boots and rubber gloves. If only I could do at least this part with my eyes shut, I thought with a sigh. But when I took another look at what remained of the arm on the board, there, where it had been severed, the pale pink meat and white, round edge of the bone suddenly turned into a Georgia O'Keefe flower.

I knelt down again and sawed off the rest of that arm at the shoulder. I had to step into the tub to get to the other one. It was a very awkward position, and twice I nicked the board with the saw.

The legs took longer. I sawed off the lower part of the leg first, then the thighbone below the hips. These bones were thick, and the saw got so hot that I had to wait for it to cool down. It was not easy to crouch over the mutilated corpse in the tub, but I tried not to think about it, to concentrate on the details – on the saw, the position of the board, the thickness of the bone. Also, my back was hurting me. This was definitely a job for a man, not a woman.

It would have been better if I had had the strength to carve up the entire corpse that day, as I had planned. But I had also intended to put the carved pieces in the refrigerator, and it was only when I started sawing that I realized how impossible that would be. The fridge was far too small to hold the entire corpse, even temporarily. So it was all the same whether I finished sawing that day or the next. I was tired and I had to dispose of at least one package that day.

When I had finished with the limbs, I had eight pieces lying on the floor, which I then divided into two piles, putting each into a black plastic rubbish bag and packing them into two sports bags by the door.

I stood under the shower. José was still lying in the tub. Without his legs he took up only three-quarters of it, so there was room for me as well. Nevertheless, I had to be careful not to step on him. I pulled the plastic shower curtain shut and let the strong jet of hot water splash on my back. The water bounced off my skin and droplets fell on to

José. With his eyes closed and wet hair clinging to his head, the scene reminded me of our morning showers together, of the moment when the first stream of water splashed on to his face. Like old times, I thought, just like old times. And then I was seized with rage. How could this mutilated corpse lying by my feet have anything to do with the living José? And why did I insist on calling him by that name, triggering off fits of stupid sentimentality? Vigorously towelling dry my hair, I thought with some resignation that in future I would simply have to avoid looking at his face. The face, still undesecrated by death, made me think of the corpse, even in its current depleted condition, as a person. This would probably last for a while yet. For these three remaining days, as long as it was physically near me, José's dead body would exist in my mind as both a person and a corpse.

That afternoon I sat on a bus and, with one of the heavy bags in my lap, set off for the Chinese restaurant on the East Side where I left the first package. It was late afternoon already and I was really tired. Returning on the subway, I was tempted to spend the rest of the day at the movies or in a bookstore, not thinking about anything, least of all the task that still lay ahead. On the way home, I saw an advertisement for *Last Tango in Paris*, which was showing at my local cinema, and as the train glided drowsily through the tunnels, I saw Marlon Brando sticking a piece of chewing gum under the balcony railing just before he was about to die. I stepped out into the street, his picture still in my mind's eye, and went into the supermarket. It was not until I put the Ajax in my basket that his face vanished. To go to the cinema in this situation was a real luxury. Instead, it would be better for me to start cleaning the apartment. I bought the detergents, a plastic brush for the floor, a few dishcloths, a window spray, chlorine and a dozen sponges.

The bedroom looked the dirtiest to me, especially the bed. There was blood on the top sheet and on one of the pillowcases. Most of it was not left by José, but by my own dirty hands. 'Bloodstains are best removed with cold water.' This sentence, printed in small type on poor quality paper, had appeared before my eyes several times already. When I became aware of it, I was not sure whether it was one of Jadwiga's stock pieces of advice, like the one counselling that after eating garlic (which is good for the flu), you should chew parsley to refresh your breath. She had had her fill of blood to clean up in our house. Before she died, my mother kept bleeding – that was one of the signs that the end was near. Since the detergent we have in Poland is of poor quality, Jadwiga had to to soak the sheets overnight in cold water first, and then boil them. So the sentence may well have been hers, but I saw it in printed form. It occurred to me that I had probably seen it at Barbara's. She used to clip practical tips out of the newspapers, such as how to remove rust stains with lemon or how to clean patent-leather shoes with milk. But this tip for blood had been tried and tested; I had followed it umpteen times washing my own underwear and sheets. Now I had to put the pillowcase and sheet in cold water, and only then launder them in the basement, where the washers and dryers were. I decided that the sheets would have to wait until I had emptied the tub of the corpse.

I moved the bed and washed the floor. This went smoothly, because the floor had a coat of brown paint on it, a colour which made it hard to see the drops of blood. I scrubbed the entire floor with a plastic brush and warm water, the way peasants do. Scrubbing on my knees, I felt it was a good thing that my day was filled with hard physical work. My mind was completely empty of thought, and that was just as well. The expression 'work therapy' popped into my mind, an image of the physical work they give the insane to do. The next few days would follow this same rhythm, and I looked forward to that.

Not to think. Not to remember.

There was no food left in the house, and there was an uncomfortable gaping void in my stomach. It was ten o'clock in the evening by the time I went to the restaurant on the corner. It was empty and the proprietor was sitting by the window looking out into the street, waiting to close up. I always saw him whenever I passed by, and I was always fascinated by his grey hair, with its tiny, evenly curled locks. He always looked as if he had just come out of the hair-dresser's. When I went in, I could barely stop myself from running my fingers through it. He smiled, as if he were reading my mind. I ordered a pork chop and a Greek salad. I immediately pounced on the bread basket. By the time my meal arrived I had already eaten all the bread, but that had not dented my appetite in the slightest. I started to chew the meat. It was neither particularly tender nor particularly tough. An ordinary, well-done pork chop, slightly bloody at the bone. I ate systematically and rather absently. I had just about finished the meal – I had picked up the bone with my fingers, because there was no other way to get to the best part – when suddenly I felt my stomach rise and vomit spewed into my plate and on to the table. Undigested pieces of grey meat and salad only just singed by stomach acid floated dolefully in the mucous which oozed slowly on to the floor. I must have looked as if I was at death's door, because the curly-haired proprietor jumped up straight away. 'Should I call an ambulance?' he asked in distress. I shook my head. I was having trouble breathing, but I felt perfectly all right. A swarthy-looking girl appeared from the kitchen, carrying a plastic basin. She took a stack of paper napkins and, without changing the expression on her face, began to clean the vomit from the table, wiping it into the basin. I got up and went into the toilet. I threw up some more in the sink, but a kind of bitter, yellowish liquid was all that remained.

I knew it was the pork that had made me sick. Not because it was bad but because I had simply overdone it with meat. During the extraordinary events of the past twenty-four hours, my body had reached a point of complete saturation, and any new morsel was like poison. I would obviously have to stop eating meat, at least for a while. Thank God the restaurant had been empty. It might have been busy; there could have been someone else sitting at my table. I could have thrown up into somebody's lap. I could not allow myself to become a social undesirable.

I gripped the sink and closed my eyes. I could feel something beyond my control happening inside me. I was not in full charge of my body. It was no longer just me. Just as sometimes I might have an absolutely certain premonition that I am going to fall ill, I knew that this vomiting episode was actually a sign of José's presence inside me.

I was changing.

My body was reacting differently now, as if every cell were in an extraordinary, different state. The only thing that troubled me was that my reactions were obviously going to be sudden and unpredictable. I might at any time do something I would not recognize as my own act. I rinsed my face. In the rusty mirror it looked calm and quite refreshed. 'Are you feeling better?' asked the proprietor, still worried, as I paid the bill.

'Thank you, I'm fine now. It's the pregnancy, you know. I should be more careful about what I eat.'

'Ah, I see, I see,' said the proprietor cheering up, his face taking on a fatherly expression.

The night air was icy and the short walk home completely restored me. Perhaps because of the approaching holiday, St Mark's Place was unusually quiet. I was sure that if I strained my ears I would be able to hear the deep, peaceful breathing of its residents. Scraps of paper and leftover food from the garbage bags rolled down the pavement; the garbage truck would not be passing until around two in the morning. A bicycle was chained firmly to the lamp-post. A taxi drove past, slowly, as if expecting me to hail it. The cars flickered by on the corner of Second Avenue.

It was a perfectly ordinary night, and somehow that was terrifying. I kicked the Coca-Cola can in my path, as if I hoped the sound would confirm I was alive.

I remembered the day my mother died. I remembered the day before, when José had died. I was petrified, and yet consoled at the same time by the idea that all days, even this one, are completely the same. There are no different days. The day of my own death will be no different from this one. Climbing up the stairs I thought of the remains in the bathtub, but the moment I touched the wooden banister I found it incredible that anything had happened at all.

When I went into the bathroom, though, there was the corpse. He was turned slightly sideways, as if the tub were too small for him. He did not look well. His skin was an unhealthy blue colour. Tomorrow, I thought, tomorrow I will finally finish this exhausting job. I went to bed. The sweetish smell of the corpse, which was starting to decompose, crept under the bathroom door and into the bedroom. Like the smell of an abattoir, I thought resignedly, and fell asleep.

In the morning the corpse looked even worse, as if blotches of spilled ink lay under his dark skin. In places the skin was turning from blue to yellowish-green, and along the sawed edges a greenish mould had started to eat away at the meat. The smell was disgusting. It was high time for me to finish sawing and dispose of all the remains. I decided to do it immediately, even before breakfast. Again I stripped naked and tied my hair back into a ponytail to keep it out of the way. I took the chopping board and laid it across the outside rim of the bathtub – naturally, I had measured the width of the tub before buying the board. Then I stood in the tub and lifted the torso on to the board. It was heavy and slippery, the position awkward. It took me three attempts to get it on properly. Just as I was about to switch on the saw and halve the torso at the waist, I remembered that I absolutely must not do that. I almost laughed at myself – what a damned amateur I was! I had remembered at the last moment that if I sawed through the torso at the waist, José's innards would spill out into the tub. And the worst thing was not that I would suddenly find myself standing in the middle of his intestines, spleen, liver, stomach and kidneys, which would be hard to scoop out from the bottom of the tub. The worst thing was that his sawn bowels would empty their contents. Shit, in other words. An incredible stench would spread from the bathroom all over the apartment and on to the staircase, and that would without doubt alarm the neighbours. I thought for a moment, and then I saw another image from my childhood. The only similar experience I had ever had was watching the pig being slaughtered in Pawlowice. I remembered that Pavel had slit the poor pig's stomach with a single cut of the knife and its entire, undamaged entrails had dropped out intact on to the frozen ground. There had been no blood, just the grey, smoking mass.

I stepped out of the tub, took the kitchen knife and, as carefully as I could, made a long incision down the torso. The knife slid smoothly; José had not an ounce of fat on him, it was all muscle. I was afraid that I might have punctured the intestines, but when I shoved my hand inside and pulled them out into the light, I saw that they were perfect. They looked like fat grey ropes, and I was surprised how long they were . The kidneys were bluish and smooth, and as I touched every part of the entrails I became aware that it was giving me pure pleasure. Because only now that José was dead could I do what I had so wanted to do when he was alive: feel him from the inside.

I placed the entrails first in one plastic bag and then in another, and tied a tight knot. Then I sawed the hollow torso in half. I immediately put the bottom half in a bag to be thrown away.

I still had to separate the head from the body, that is from this now completely shapeless hunk of meat which had a head stuck on top of it. If I could just concentrate on this remaining piece of the corpse lying on the blood-stained chopping board, just as it would have been in the pathology department of a hospital; if I could concentrate on it as if it were the remains of an abstract corpse, then the task would not seem so difficult. But whenever I happened to catch sight of his face, of his head, I flinched. Twice I switched on the saw, but when I brought the blade close to his neck, my hand would stop. What was it exactly that was stopping me from pressing the saw against his neck? It was the idea that separating the head from the body was the final parting with José. As long as the smallest piece of his body was near me, in the tub or in the refrigerator, within arm's reach, so to speak, I felt that we had not completely separated. I knew that it would be easier for me if we did not have to part in such a hurry. I needed time to adjust psychologically to this new situation. Everything was happening too quickly.

I took José's box of Gitanes and his purple lighter from the kitchen table and lit myself a cigarette. The last time I had done that was almost twenty years ago at a school celebration. It was winter, I remember, and two girls from my class and I were standing in the toilet puffing smoke out of the open window and coughing. The cigarette had a burning taste which I could not wash out of my mouth for days. And it was the same now. I opened the kitchen window and blew out the smoke which burned my throat. The outside of the windowpane was covered with a grey film of sticky smog. There is still that to do, I thought angrily and flicked the unfinished cigarette down into the back alley. I could not allow myself the luxury of being paralyzed by uncontrolled emotions and sudden mood swings. I picked up a tea towel and put it over José's face.

After that I had no further problems. I switched the saw back on and made the last short incision. I wrapped the head in the tea towel and put it in the freezer compartment of the refrigerator. I sawed the rest of the torso in two. It looked like two ordinary good-sized pieces of veal. They did not digust me at all. I wrapped them up and put them in the fridge as well, because I could not carry everything away at once. And I wanted them out of the way while I cleaned up the apartment. The bathroom was in a mess, but at last it was empty.

Scrubbing the bathtub, tiles, floor and sink with a

lemon-scented greenish detergent, I turned up the radio. Vivaldi's *Four Seasons* cheerfully echoed through the apartment. A bit more and it will all be done, I told myself. I stripped the sheet off the bed and soaked it in cold water. With happy anticipation, I remembered that the following day would be Christmas Eve.

I had left Christmas Eve for myself. I awoke late, around noon. I was feeling good. The apartment was clean – I had finished the kitchen the previous day. José was finally 'buried', that is to say, his remains had been distributed between various city rubbish dumps. The bed linen and towels, even the tea towels (except for the one in which I had wrapped José's head) were dry and neatly put away in the cupboard, and there were only my suitcases to close. I could devote my time to myself without feeling guilty about it.

First I lolled around in bed for a while, had my coffee, and leafed through two fashion magazines I had bought the night before on my way home from Battery Park, where I had left the last package in one of the dumpsters. There was still the head, which I had frozen. I planned to take that with me to the airport and find a convenient place to leave it. I had bought *Vogue* and *Elle* as presents for myself for a job well done. I enjoyed the idea of waking up in the morning in a warm bed and reading articles about what men think about the return of the mini-skirt or what to wear on New Year's Eve. Reading women's magazines was not an indulgence exclusive to Barbara. Once or twice a year I too would wistfully skim through the silky pages of foreign fashion magazines, not because I wanted anything in particular (on the contrary, I wanted everything, from underwear to shoes and perfume), but because these picture books for grown-up women opened the door to a world of fairytales.

I ran myself a bubble bath. That is what the magazines said: after a hard day's work, treat yourself to a luxurious bubble bath. It was one treat I could give myself. It was only as I relaxed into the hot water that I felt how stiff my muscles were. Inside my body, my changed body, I felt a tension which came not only from physical exertion and fatigue, but from a keen, hypertrophied awareness of the body which I had endured for the last few days now. The tight coil ran from my neck and shoulders along my limbs, all the way down to the tips of my toes. At the same time, my other body seemed supple and light, like the body of a ballerina. When I closed my eyes, it was like being in a tunnel. Parts of that tunnel were my arms, my legs, my head. The tunnel was not completely dark – light seeped in from all sides, just as if it were penetrating my skin. As I travelled, I recognized the heart, the stomach, the kidneys, the veins and muscles, even the cells. Roaming around my own insides, I became aware that my every cell was soaked with José. A wave of contentment washed over me.

He was mine. We were one.

The tip from *Elle* worked. I was relaxed and full of energy, as if José and I had just made love. He would usually fall asleep or doze off immediately afterwards, and I always wondered what made men so tired, even when they had made love for barely five minutes. How was it that they got so physically exhausted? Making love always drained him and gave me strength. I would lie there next to him, my eyes open, more awake than ever. Even when I was tired or sleepy, making love always perked me up. I felt like getting up and running around or dancing. When I stepped out of the bath, that is exactly how I felt, refreshed and full of unexpected energy.

José had taught me finally to like my body, and his death

would not change that. From now on I would love my body, and him inside it, even more.

I shampooed my hair thoroughly and then rinsed it with vinegar water. I combed it out, dried it with a hairdrier, and then rubbed moisturizing cream on my body. But when I bent down to pick up a few hairs that had fallen on the floor, I was gripped by an uneasiness. There was no particular reason for it, because I had already washed the floor, but it occurred to me that maybe it was not clean enough. It was a typically neurotic reaction: I took a Q-tip, dipped it in diluted alcohol and knelt on the floor. I simply had to clean the gaps between the bathroom tiles. Then I went into the bedroom and did the same between the floorboards. I worked until my back started aching and it was time to get ready for midnight mass.

I knew that in these four days, my idea of cleanliness had turned into an obsessive, self-punishing activity. I was perfectly aware that something else was involved here, a subconscious desire to atone for sin. It emerged only now, when everything was finished already and when, for the first time in those four days, I had time to myself.

It might appear again, I thought, this idea of sin. But there had been no sin, there could not be. Not for a single moment could I allow myself to think that I had committed a sin. That would be tantamount to suicide. There was no difference, there could be no difference, between the survivors in the Andes and me.

I put on a dark red lipstick. I liked the contrast between the bright lips and the pale hair. All I had to do now was dress. I put on my new black dress, which covered everything but hugged the hips. I looked just the way I wanted to, like a real widow.

It was snowing heavily outside. The snow had already

blanketed the street and covered the footprints of the people who had already made their way to church. Walking on the thin silvery carpet of snow, I felt as if I were the first person ever to walk this path. Alone as never before in my life, I stepped through the ethereal white landscape of this wild city in the silence of Christmas Eve night. As I approached the church, I heard organ music.

I felt blessed.

New life flickered inside me.

It was Christmas Day, at last. The taxi taking me to the airport drove along the deserted avenues where the snow had already turned to slush. Here and there, we would pass some small, dark figure treading carefully on the icy sidewalk. New York was still asleep, like a fat cat. Through the rear window of the cab, I watched the city recede. As we crossed the Triborough Bridge, Manhattan grew smaller and smaller. I was strangely unmoved, drained of all feeling. New York without José meant no more to me than a colourful picture postcard. One day I might find just such a card in my mailbox in Warsaw.

Who knows what I would think then, and what I would remember.

I had put the cardboard box on the seat next to me. Inside was a round cookie tin I had found in the pantry. We used it mostly for flour. I had poured the remains of the flour into the kitchen sink, removed José's head from the freezer and, wrapped in its tea towel, placed it inside the tin.

At the terminal I first checked in my two heavy suitcases. I still had just over an hour before the flight and I had to get rid of the box. Of course, I could not take it with me through the scanner into the transit lounge, so I had to

206

leave it somewhere. I took an airport bus to the next terminal. Before disposing of the box, I wanted to take one
last look at José. I did not want to admit it to myself, but I
could not part with him just like that, without a backward
glance, without saying goodbye.

The only place where I could unwrap the head was in
the toilet. But in America toilets are divided merely by
flimsy partitions which do not reach up to the ceiling or
down to the floor, and which provide no privacy whatsoever. When I went into the ladies' toilet, I saw one solitary
pair of female legs under the partition. The other cubicles
were empty. Obviously, I did not think that some woman
was going to climb on to the toilet seat and peek over the
partition, but nonetheless I felt unsure of myself, exposed,
with the box in my hand.

I knew there was no point in opening it, because it was
not José any more. It could not be anything any more but
a piece of meat which, after four days, I would be better off
not seeing. But the urge was so strong that I untied the
string, opened the box and took out the head. I had to be
careful not to get myself dirty while unwrapping it, so I
placed it on the closed toilet seat and knelt on the floor.
The tea towel was still frozen and stiff. It wouldn't come off
easily: I had to peel it slowly from the skull. Finally, I uncov-
ered the face. There was no skin left on it any more. The
frozen pieces had stuck to the towel. The naked, black-
ened meat on José's cheeks and forehead looked like
burns. The ice was already starting to melt, and a thick
liquid was appearing on the surface of the wounds, slowly
dripping on to the towel. A lock of hair had come off with
the towel, revealing a pale piece of skull above the brow.
José's entire face had decomposed into a shapeless, swollen
mass of ice. His perfectly shaped lips were now a dark blue

gash in the bloated flesh which looked just like bile. I was taken aback by the speed with which José had decomposed and turned into a pulpy mass. Into slime. Into nothing.

No, I didn't need this, I thought, furious at my own stupidity. This had been unwarranted.

Although I realized that it was absolutely idiotic, nonetheless I leaned over and brushed my lips against the spot where his mouth had been only the other day. Then I wrapped up the head again and flushed the toilet. I found a garbage can in one of the corridors and dropped the box into it. Then I took the airport bus back to my terminal. They were announcing the last call for Lot passengers to Warsaw, and I hurried toward my gate.

Disencumbered, I entered the plane.

My lips were still burning from José's icy kiss.

XIII

The plane has been flying over the ocean for some time now, but I still cannot sleep. I am so tired I was sure I would fall asleep as soon as the plane hit the sky above New York. I had dinner – they served pork in a brown sauce of indeterminate taste, and mashed potatoes. Needless to say, I tried to order a vegetarian meal, but Lot does not cater for such requirements, not even on a flight from America. So I just ate the mashed potatoes and cabbage salad. I drank a glass of white wine with it, to soften the fall of the food in my stomach. It is Christmas, which is why the plane is half empty. The interior is now plunged in darkness, the movie screen providing the only light. I do not have headphones and so I am guessing what the actors are saying. It is more fun that way anyway. I hear only the smooth hum of the engines and the occasional snoring of the man to my right. His head keeps lolling toward me, and his breath smells of vodka. Maybe that's the best way, to down two or three vodkas to make the trip go faster. For me it is going slowly. Suddenly, I wish I were already in Warsaw. I am tired of America, of my life there. I am lucky that the seat to my left is vacant – at least I can put my feet up.

Behind me somebody is chattering softly in Polish. I make myself comfortable and pull my blanket over me. An occasional star slips past the pitch blackness clinging to the window. I am warm and cosy. I can feel myself start to relax. I find the whispering behind me pleasant, a woman's voice and a man's. I cannot tell what they are talking about, but their voices have the effect of a lullaby. I feel good like this. Soon I will settle down and fall asleep. For the first time in a month I feel content somehow, at peace with myself.

Finally, half asleep, I can feel myself floating between two worlds. One is already behind me, the other is still far away. My departure from New York closes a stage of my life. I have to admit that I have never felt so whole, so completely fulfilled. I will be thirty soon. In the spring I will defend my doctoral thesis on English metaphysical poets. I will continue to work at the institute – this trip was only a short, three-month break. And I will continue to live in the small apartment of my late aunt. Friends might say I have changed, but I know that none of them will see what I see in my face. That it is all over already, finished. Everything that can ever happen in life has happened to me. Only a careful, experienced eye might notice peace reflected in my expression, the kind of peace that radiates from the faces of the very old, which at first glance may look vacuous. The kind of peace we find in sick people who unexpectedly recover from some dangerous, deadly disease. It is the peace that comes with the presence of death. I saw it in my own face this morning, when I cast a last glance in the bathroom mirror of my New York apartment. I stood there, in that impeccably clean bathroom, and suddenly in the mirror I noticed the trace of death in the corners of my mouth, on my forehead, in the gaze of my eyes. It did not frighten me – quite the opposite, I even smiled at myself. Why, just a few moments ago, when I was in the aeroplane toilet, I looked in the mirror and assured myself once again that to a superficial eye I radiate contentment and self-confidence.

No, nobody will ever see on my face what has happened in my life in these past few months.

Now I am flying ten thousand metres above the Atlantic Ocean and there is no other reality but this one. The smell of stale air, the drone of the plane engine, the voices and feeling of comfort. I need nothing more to feel the certainty of existence. In about five hours I will be in Warsaw. There my old life awaits me. I will slip into it as into a shabby housedress which still carries the smell of soap, dust and parquet polish. In the old world memories of the new world will completely fade, like an over-exposed photograph. I will forget, I will forget everything that is unimportant.

Except for what I carry inside me.

The smell on my hands is all that is left to remind me of New York. They still reek of the ammonia I used to clean the tiles. I should have used rubber gloves, but it is too late to think about that now. My nails are cracked and my fingertips are rough from detergent. Every so often I rub Vaseline on my hands, but it will be a few days before they look normal again. The smell of ammonia is unpleasant. Just when I am trying to relax and go to sleep, it keeps taking me back to the apartment in New York and to what happened there.

Why? Why did I do it? I cannot answer that question properly, even now that it is all over. I only know that I could not have done otherwise. I did not want to lose him. José belonged to me alone, and I simply wanted it to stay that way, to possess him totally, forever. Before I met him I knew nothing about real love, the kind where everything is possible, everything is allowed, even death. Love gives a person absolute power over another human being. I merely took full advantage of that.

And he is here, inside me, enclosed forever in my body, in my every cell. He lives inside me. He touches with my hands, breathes with my breath, sees through my eyes.

It's odd. It is barely four days since José died, yet to me it seems so long ago. As if, by moving away from New York, I am also moving away from my life with him. And now, as I fly toward Warsaw, I feel that I would be happiest if I could forget everything, everything except the awareness of his presence inside me. But when I raise my hands to my face, images of our life together flash through my mind. It hurts; for now it still hurts.

But in time the pain will evaporate, just like the smell.